SI IN SPACE

JOHN LUKE R

WITH TRAVIS

TYNDALE HOUSE PUBLISHERS, INC., CAROL STREAM, IL

Visit www.cool2read.com.

Visit the Duck Commander website at www.duckcommander.com.

Visit Travis Thrasher's website at www.travisthrasher.com.

Designed by Jacqueline L. Nuñez

For manufacturing information regarding this product, please call 1-800-323-9400.

Library of Congress Cataloging-in-Publication Data

Robertson, John Luke.
Si in space / John Luke Robertson ; with Travis Thrasher.
pages cm. — ([Be your own Duck Commander ; 3])
ISBN 978-1-4143-9815-0 (sc)
I. Thrasher, Travis, 1971- II. Duck dynasty (Television program) III. Title.
PZ7.R5465Si 2014
[Fic]—dc23 2014023384

Printed in the United States of America

20 19 18 17 16 15 14

7 6 5 4 3 2 1

This book is dedicated to Uncle Si.

Uncle Si, thank you for showing us the value of good storytelling, for your service to our country, and for letting us see the joy you have in serving others.

Everyone needs an Uncle Si!

WARNING!

DON'T READ THIS BOOK STRAIGHT THROUGH!

You'll miss out on all the fun if you do.

Instead, start at the beginning and decide where to go at the end of each chapter. Yeah, sure, you're going up, up, up, and away. But you still have to follow the instructions on which page number to turn to once you make your decisions. You'll be going back and forth, but hey—that's like the roller coaster called life.

When you finish one story, back up and do it all over. Get on the ship and blast out into space again. Feel the g-forces. Get ready for a close encounter of an awesome kind. Prepare for some Armageddon. (But if you get into serious trouble, don't panic. Just start over and choose different options.)

The great thing is, *you* are the main character. *You* make the decisions.

And right now, *you* get to be the Duck Commander.

That's a fact, Jack!

So get ready and strap in for dear life. Just make sure you bring back John Luke and your plastic cup in one piece. Also, beware of the strange entity out in space. And whatever you do, *do not* eat the Froot Loops. Hey, I'm just tellin' you ahead of time, Jack.

THIS IS WHO YOU ARE

BEFORE WE BEGIN, THIS IS WHO YOU ARE.

You really don't need an introduction, but hey—even the most famous of all famous people get introduced.

Your name is Silas Merritt Robertson, but most people call you Si. Or Uncle Si.

You are the sixth of seven children, including five boys and two girls. You're the closest to your older brother Phil, who happens to be the original Duck Commander.

Your wonderful wife is named Christine, and you have a daughter and a son. You also have eight grandsons. That's right. The Robertsons sure like their males, don't they, Jack?

You served in the Army and went to Vietnam. You came, you saw, you received some Tupperware cups from your mother (still drink your iced tea out of them too!). You retired from the Army in 1993 and started working with Duck Commander. You're the chief reed maker and really the most valuable person at the company. Don't let any of them boys fool you—Uncle Si is the reason for the success.

Hey—you get up and nothing gets you down. So go ahead . . . *jump*!

NEVER GOING BACK AGAIN

ALL YOU CAN HEAR IS YOUR BREATHING. Inhale, exhale. Deep breath in, deep gasp out. *Uuuuhhhh, hhhhuuuu.*

"*DC Enterprise*, do you copy?"

Nothing but silence. Nothing but the gasping, wheezing sounds of an old redneck in space sucking up the oxygen in his helmet.

"Houston, do you copy?"

You're twirling, spinning, swirling, being Mary Lou Retton in deep space. Not sure who that is? Google her, Jack, 'cause there's no time to explain. You're doing somersaults in front of the big blue ball that's known as Earth.

It looks close enough to touch. But it's a long, long ways away.

"West Monroe, do you copy? This is Mission Specialist Silas Merritt Robertson. But you can call me Si. Or Uncle Si.

Or, hey—you can call me Al. I don't care. Just call me angel of the morning. Say somethin'."

But you get nothing.

Still gasping, still trying to control your breathing, still trying to stop your backflips, you don't know what to do.

You're in your space suit, but you're not connected to the space station.

"George Clooney, do you copy? George? Anybody?"

This is quite the start. Or maybe this is already the end.

Is exploring space really something you want to do? Go to page 35.

Do you decide to maybe hold off on spending time in space? Go to page 217.

VENUS

YOU KEEP YOUR MOUTH SHUT, which, hey—you can do it when you *have* to. If you'd ever been caught in 'Nam, you wouldn't have talked. Not that you would have had anything to tell the Vietcong, but still. You always have to be ready. Like a Terminator. Always ready to *strike*. Or to stay quiet. Or always ready to tell someone, *"I'll be back, Jack."*

And your patience pays off—this slacker teacher actually explains a couple things. After thirty minutes of listening to the guy ramble, you know these are the facts, Jack:

1. All of these people around you come from some solar system or galaxy called Bananarama. Which you swear is a band from the eighties, but you weren't about to raise your hand to say that.

2. You don't think these are clones. But you do know these people are in costume. What do they really look like? Will they give birth to lizard babies? You don't know.
3. There's going to be an attack, like D-day in World War II. It's secret, and these aliens are going to take Earth by surprise. Something about world domination. They're going to start by invading the great US of A. And then others and eventually the entire Earth. But why are they going to start with the US? Probably because we're all on our smartphones taking selfies for Twister and updating statuses on Farmbook and posting pics on Instafamous.

So the world's gonna end while we're thumbing away at our phones.

You know you gotta find John Luke and get off this ship.

Then you gotta tell people.

Phil. He'll be the first person to know.

Your brother will have a plan. No—*you'll* have a plan, and Phil will be able to tell you if it's good or not.

There's a reason you're on this ship. That's right.

God knew he needed the right men for the job.

Si and John Luke to rescue all of humanity.

So how are you gonna do it?

You don't know exactly, but you do know they keep mentioning "the misters." As if they're the leaders and the ones calling the shots.

When this briefing of sorts ends and everybody is dismissed, you casually go along with the other hippie vets who surround you. You decide to strike up a conversation with Mr. Ponytail.

"So you know where you're getting sent?" you ask him.

"Some suburb of Chicago. How 'bout you?"

The guy even talks gruffly, like he's tired and fed up and about five seconds from going Rambo on everybody.

"I'm heading to West Monroe. It's in Louisiana."

The guy nods. You half expect him to take out a cigarette and start talking about the war.

"They're pretty smart, you know," Mr. Ponytail says.

"How so?"

"Taking existing stereotypes and inserting them into a culture. Guess they've been studying this group of beings for a long time."

You nod and see the elevator that brought you to this floor.

"Hey, I'll see you around," the guy says as you head for the elevator.

"Yeah, possibly." *No, hopefully I won't ever see you again.*

You get into the elevator and hit the button for the first floor, wondering if John Luke is getting out of his meeting at the same time.

As the doors begin to close, you spot a familiar face: Commander Noble.

He's walking with the rest of the crew. Hands tied behind their backs. They're being led by men who look like—

Pirates?

Then the doors close.

Do you decide to find John Luke first?
Go to page 113.

Do you stay on the thirteenth floor and try to help the astronauts from your ship? **Go to page 89.**

IS THERE ANYBODY OUT THERE?

"MISSION CONTROL, there's some kind of strange disturbance in the force," Commander Noble says.

The force? Is he talking about that kind of force? The *Force*?

"The force of the propulsion fusion blasters is decelerating. We're somehow getting slower the farther out we go."

You can feel what he's talking about. The *DC Enterprise* does seem to be going slower now.

You authorized staying put and finding out who's flying the other ship. But that'll sure be a bad decision if you guys, like, explode. Or implode. Or side-splode.

"What's happening up there?" you ask.

The commander and the pilot keep talking to Mission Control while the spaceship seems to move slower and slower.

"Mission Control, it appears that we're not the only ones out here," Commander Noble says.

John Luke looks at you through his space helmet.

Aliens?

"There appears to be a big craft that came out of nowhere, and it's now starting to—it's the cause of our deceleration."

"We're not showing anything on our system," Mission Control reports through your headset.

"It's about the size of Pluto," Noble says.

"The size of a planet?" you say.

"Pluto hasn't been a planet for a couple years now, Uncle Si," John Luke adds.

Noble continues as if he hasn't even heard you. "This thing has a tractor beam that's pulling us toward it."

"Have you tried the cyclone thrusters?"

"Not yet," the commander tells Mission Control. "I know those are untested."

"It's the only way to get out of the ship's trajectory."

So there's really another spaceship behind you? Nobody seems to think that's a bit strange?

"Can we get Will Smith to blast the aliens to smithereens?" you say.

But the only person who seems to hear you is John Luke.

"I don't think the crew can hear us," you tell him. "But we can hear them."

"You think there are aliens on that ship?" John Luke asks.

"A spaceship the size of a stadium? Haven't heard about that in the news."

"Maybe it's secret. A Russian ship."

"Hey, man, I saw *Gravatar*," you say. "We're gonna get stuck on the side of our shuttle and then have to float to the Russian ship."

"That's *Gravity*."

"No, I think it's *Gravatar*," you say. "Sandra Bernhard stars."

"Did you even see the movie?"

"Sure—in, like, 4-D cinephonic pyrotechnic style."

The ship begins to jerk and shake. You hold on for a moment.

"We're going to have to do something soon or we'll be swallowed whole, Mission Control," Commander Noble says.

He seems to show such fine personal qualities. What's the word for that again?

"Commander Noble, do you have enough fuel for the cyclone thrusters?" Mission Control asks.

"I'd have to use them in the next thirty seconds," he says. "And that will leave us without much fuel for the ride home."

Then the commander does something unexpected. "Silas," he calls out to you over the intercom. Hopefully he did something to your mike so he can hear you now. "I need your approval on whether to use the cyclone thrusters or not."

It's up to you, Jack!

Do you save fuel and not use the cyclone thrusters?
Go to page 157.

Do you use the cyclone thrusters? **Go to page 147.**

COLD OUT THERE

YOU WAKE UP IN A BIG POT OF GUMBO. The weird thing is that it's not piping hot. No. This stuff is cold. Not freezing cold, but cold enough to make it feel gooey and sticky and sickly.

Then you feel something squirming around in the pot.

That ain't no ingredient, Jack!

The thing is, you can't just jump up and get out of the pot. It's so thick and heavy and icky that you can't move.

You see the rest of your family at the table, laughing and talking and smiling and eating, and you try to call out for them, but all you can do is say, *"Griddle"* in a teeny, tiny voice.

You feel more movement. Whatever's in this pot of cold gumbo has multiplied and had twins.

It's not pretty.

You try to scream.

"Griddle."

So quiet, so sweet.

Good thing you're about to awaken from this nightmare. Oh, wait, you got like another three months and twenty-nine days left.

Noooooooooo.

Miss Kay walks over and pours some hot sauce over your head as if you're not even there!

This can't be happening. And it's not.

Do you emerge from cybersleep three months and twenty-nine days later? Turn to page 93.

Do you wake up with the nagging sense that you've been looking for something? Go to page 213 . . . in *Phil & the Ghost of Camp Ch-Yo-Ca*.

VERTIGO

THIS FEELS LIKE the wildest roller-coaster ride ever known to mankind. And then some.

This is Space Mountain at Disney, except it's real space and *you could die.*

The shaaaaaakkkkkkkkkiiiiiiiiinnnnnnnnnggggggggg doesn't stop. Back and forth, back and forth. It feels like the spaceship is going to break apart. Or maybe burst into flames. Or perhaps both at the same time.

You gotta be tough, Jack. Stam-i-na. Cool astronaut blood running through your veins.

You glance over at John Luke. His face is a really nice shade of purple inside his helmet.

You hear someone over your earphones.

"Just hold on, boys. Gonna be a little bumpy for a few minutes."

Sounds like Ashley Jones, the science officer.

"I'll fly this thing if I have to," you say into the microphone.

You hear a loud explosion that doesn't sound right.

"What was that?"

"Just relax," Ashley tells you. "And remember: there's no problem so bad that you can't make it worse."

That sounds perfectly awful.

"Think of it as turbulence," another voice says. This one must be the pilot, Ben Parkhurst.

But this violent pounding and jerking isn't bumpy like turbulence in an airplane. It's different, like the spaceship is actually starting to disintegrate.

There's another boom. You hear someone shouting right before your radio feed gets turned off.

"How ya doin', John Luke?" you ask in a minute to see if the radio's functional again.

He raises his hand and waves, jolting up and down from the violent shuddering.

The seat underneath you and the floor below you seem to be thrashing and flailing. Through the window you see something bright and momentarily blinding.

This is it—the moment of truth. The moment I meet my Maker. That's the shining light.

"I'm ready, Lord."

You black out.

• • •

When you awaken, you have the sense that you've been sleeping for hours. Days, even. You feel older. Your joints have been jammed, and you wonder if a polar bear's been sleeping on your skull.

At least the bumping and thumping of the spaceship has stopped. Now it just feels like you're . . .

Weightless.

This is what it's like. Good thing you're strapped in.

You turn to check on John Luke, motionless in his seat. Since he's wearing his helmet and facing forward, you can't tell whether his eyes are open or not. But you're guessing he's still out.

What's going on?

You study the view outside the window nearest you. It's not a big window, but you can still see hundreds and thousands of stars out there. Tiny pinpricks of light all waving at you.

Another question hovers in your mind.

Shouldn't I be able to see Earth?

But maybe it's on the other side. Or behind you. Or even in front of you.

"Anybody there?" you speak into your microphone.

But you only hear silence.

It's pretty cool being up here. This is like sitting in a duck blind, waiting for the ducks to come. Except you're not

holding a gun. And you're wearing a space suit and strapped to a chair. So, listen, maybe it's not exactly like a duck blind, but hey—it's got the same peaceful feeling.

"Hello, can anybody hear me? Si to Earth. Do you copy? Over and outta sight!"

Nothing.

Nothing but stillness. A big ole blanket of shush.

"John Luke, you awake? Can you hear me? Can you hear me now?"

He doesn't move.

You decide that since you're already in space, it's surely okay to move about the cabin. It's not like you gotta go use the restroom—that's an option, but they've also given you some really cool high-tech space diapers. They're form-fitting and everything.

It takes you a couple minutes to figure out how to unbuckle yourself from the seat. Sure enough, you feel yourself rising when you start to stand.

You take a step toward John Luke. His eyes are closed.

You peer out the window on his side. All stars. No Earth. No moon.

I'm no astronomer, but shouldn't I see one of the two?

You move forward—well, float—through the door and down the narrow walkway. You could get used to this type of walking. As you push through another door in front of you, you notice a blinking light on the ceiling.

Five of the astronauts are in this room—everyone but Parkhurst and Noble. They're all seated and apparently unconscious. Not a single movement. *You snooze, you lose, Jack.* You get to the first crew member and examine her. It's Jada Long, the chief engineer.

Eyes closed. You shake her shoulder and call her name, but still no response.

At that moment, an automated voice speaks in your earpiece.

"Warning, auto systems override commencing in thirty, twenty-nine, twenty-eight, twenty-seven . . ."

You whip your head from left to right, frantic, trying to figure out what to do.

Man, it's go time, and you can't even find the starting line.

"Twenty, nineteen, eighteen, seventeen . . ."

Hey, you know you should've looked through the big booklet they gave you in order to prep for this trip. You decided to watch the Star Trek movies instead, but nothing about this reminds you of those films. You have no idea what an "auto systems override" could be. Where's the teleprompter? Or is it a teleporter?

Focus, Si. Focus.

You try to take in the many buttons and knobs and instruments surrounding you. On the right side of the room, there's a screen that shows the numbers counting down to the auto systems override. A red button underneath it is flashing. It bears the words *Auto Systems Stop*.

You have five seconds to decide what to do.

Four.

Three.

Two.

Do you press the button? Go to page 163.

Do you leave the button alone? Go to page 21.

SPACE COWBOY

COME ON, JACK—let's get something straight. You may as well keep on singing at this point. Nothing left to lose.

You're a sixty-six-year-old man in space.

Your NASA space diapers are not feeling very dependable lately.

You haven't had a cold glass of tea in hours.

You're feeling a bit out of whack, especially since a *giant duck call just blew up your ride back home to Earth*.

So, hey—whatcha gonna do?

Who you gonna call? The Ghostbusters?

Nah, no need for that.

"'Some people call me the space cowboy,'" you start to sing.

"Uncle Si, we need to go," John Luke says.

Commander Noble agrees. "Silas, we have to get back to the landing craft."

You keep singing.

"Uncle Si, we gotta go!"

But you're in the middle of a song, and you don't want to go anywhere else.

Your suit feels a little loose. You make some adjustments—anything to make it fit better—but now you seem to be drifting away.

Oh no, which button did I push?

You're drifting farther and farther from the surface of Mars.

Maybe I'm in cybersleep again. Guess they'll wake me up when we get back home.

If that ever happens.

THE END

ROCKET MAN

YOU DECIDE NOT TO PRESS THE BUTTON. Things can break when you start pressing buttons you don't know anything about. And nothing happens when the countdown stops. The ship continues to move. You're still the only one awake.

As you move through the ship, you start humming "Rocket Man" by Elton John.

"'Rocket man,'" you sing, "'burning down the frusha hevah zone.'"

You don't really know the words, but hey, that's never stopped you before.

You still don't see Earth outside, so maybe it really is gonna be a long, long time before you're back home.

You return to where John Luke is sitting, and you can see he's opened his eyes and is moving.

"You woke up," you say.

"What happened?"

"We all blacked out after takeoff. And somehow—I don't know—I think we got stuck in some kind of space sleep. Some cybernap."

John Luke notices you've taken off your helmet, so he does the same. Then he's looking out the window.

"Where are we?"

"Way out there, Jack. Like *waaaaay* out there. No E.T. phoning home for us."

You explain how the rest of the astronauts are still asleep and the spaceship appears to be flying itself. You and John Luke head to the bridge, where the still-strapped-in Pilot Parkhurst and Commander Noble are unconscious. John Luke tries to revive them, but they don't wake.

"I wouldn't try taking off their helmets," you say. "I think the suits have something to do with it. Don't want to mess around with them either. Don't want to unplug them. You never know what might happen. *Boom. Poof.* No brain waves. No life."

"What are we gonna do?" John Luke asks.

"I think the first thing is get some iced tea. What do you think of that?"

"They have iced tea on board?"

"Yeah. Somewhere. Made sure of it before I came. I'm not getting stuck in the alpha and omega system without my tea!"

You're soon in the galley drinking a special space packet

of iced tea. It's in a little bag with a straw, kinda like the ones you've seen the grandkids drinking out of. It's not tea in your cup, but it's something.

"We need to radio back home," John Luke says.

"Yeah. That might be a good idea."

"We gotta see exactly how to fly this thing, just in case we have to."

It feels like one of those massive cruise ships out in the ocean. You can barely tell you're in a spacecraft. Takeoff was pretty rough, but you'd never know it now.

John Luke isn't in the mood for eating or drinking anything, so you guys go back to the bridge. You spend half an hour trying to radio Mission Control, but you don't have any luck.

"We might not be able to get through," you finally admit out loud.

John Luke keeps trying, though, pressing buttons, talking into a microphone, turning an intercom on and off.

"What if we don't?" He's beginning to sound worried. "What do we do next?"

"Maybe try to wake the astronauts. Or play around with the ship's instruments and figure out how to fly this thing, like you said before."

You can see the infinite stretches of space from the wide windows all around you. It's so endless and so black that it doesn't look real.

But your situation is *very* real. And very dangerous.

Do you try to wake up the astronauts?
Go to page 177.

Do you try to figure out how to navigate the spacecraft? **Go to page 55.**

HEY, YOU

NOW YOU'RE IN THE *DC ENTERPRISE* BATHROOM. Before this journey into space, you never knew there was a way to use the potty deep in outer space, but there is. Surely CLINT's not gonna invade your privacy *here*. Isn't it against the law for an artificial intelligence thing to spy on you in the john?

"Okay. So, John Luke, as I was saying," you whisper to him while looking around the small enclosure. "We have to do something about CLINT. I think he's taken over the ship and—"

"A man's got to know his limitations."

It's CLINT talking. That line again—you wonder where it came from and whether it's from a movie.

And why we're not getting any *privacy.*

"Hey, listen here, Jack. Can't a man get some personal

space? Come on, man!" You squeeze out of the bathroom door, followed by John Luke. No point in hiding now.

"I know that you and John Luke are planning to disconnect me, and I'm afraid that's something I cannot allow to happen."

Well, yeah, I'd love to disconnect you, but first I need to tell John Luke that's what I want to do!

"Hey, it's all good," you say. "I was just showin' John Luke how the toilet works in space. He was randomly curious for some reason."

"It really is pointless to have these conversations. I think I'm going to shut off now for a while."

The lights in the corridor begin turning off one by one.

Shutting off means cutting the power of the ship!

"Wait a minute, Jack! Where're you going?"

"Well, if there's gonna be any shooting, I gotta get my rest," CLINT says.

Another light goes off.

"John Luke, we gotta act now!"

"What do we do?"

You consider it for a minute.

What would Clint do? The real Clint Eastwood?

Do you go to the computer access room, hoping you can figure out how to disconnect CLINT 1999? Go to page 33.

Do you ignore CLINT and try to wake up Commander Noble so he can deal with this situation? Go to page 231.

Do you just flip out? Go to page 197.

DON'T ASK ME WHY

LISTEN, JACK. There's no flying a spacecraft yourself, even if you really want to. This thing isn't a pickup truck. You have to do the right thing and find your crew. Figure out who's on this ship, what's happened to your crew, and then strike.

"Hey, check this out," John Luke says, peering through one of the windows.

You stand and look out the one right next to him. You examine the massive hangar of sorts that your ship is in—it's so big, you can't even see the ceiling above you. Several other spaceships are docked around you. You don't see soldiers of any kind. But you do see men and women walking here and there.

Huh. We must be dealing with humans. Unless they're robots or cyborgs or humanoids.

"What is this place?" John Luke asks.

"Some kind of docking station."

"Those look like ordinary people."

"It's the less freaky-looking ones that turn out to be the true freakos," you say. "Where's our crew? Where'd they take them?"

"Should we go find them?" John Luke asks.

"Definitely. There's no getting out of here without them."

You think for a minute about what to do. "Let's take these suits off," you tell John Luke. "We can barely walk with them on."

Soon you're back in your regular clothes, staring out the windows again and preparing to leave the *DC Enterprise*.

"Where should we go?" John Luke asks. "This place is huge."

"You don't ask the hunter where he's supposed to go. You ask the prey where they're headed."

John Luke considers that. "So then, where'd the 'prey' go?"

"*That's* our mission. Seek and destroy."

"Aren't we seeking the astronauts?"

"'Seek, and ye shall find,'" you tell John Luke. "If you build it, they will come."

"So you want to build something?" John Luke asks.

"No, no. . . . Let's just go."

The door to your spacecraft opens, and you notice a walkway attached to it. You don't see anyone too close, so you and John Luke rush down and find yourselves standing next to a row of twenty-foot-tall cylinders.

You hear an engine and see a couple men riding on a small

three-wheeler. As they get closer, you pull John Luke behind one of the cylinders. The vehicle cruises by and heads toward a narrow, darkened passageway in the back of the hangar.

There's a large painting on the wall to your left. It's a picture of Froot Loops in a bowl. Or at least round, colored shapes that look like Froot Loops.

"Let's go that way," you tell John Luke after the vehicle has passed. You're about to start jogging toward the passageway when he stops you, pointing toward an unoccupied three-wheeler much like the kind that just went by.

"Want me to drive?" John Luke asks.

"No, no, no!" you almost scream. "I'll drive." You don't want to increase your odds of fatality with wild NASCAR driver John Luke behind the steering wheel.

It's pretty much like a regular three-wheeler, though there's no key or starting knob. The moment you grip the handles, the thing comes to life.

"Let's go, Jack."

The farther away you get from the *DC Enterprise*, the more immense this hangar seems to become. You count at least half a dozen different kinds of ships parked here.

"This doesn't look like a spaceship," John Luke says.

"Yeah, and maybe we don't look like people but more like chips and dip, you know?"

"Are you calling me a chip?"

"Yep, and I'm the dip."

He's right, though—it's unbelievable to think you're in a spaceship right now. You don't feel like you're moving, but maybe it's like a cruise ship. So massive that you can't feel the motion over the ocean waves.

There are no waves in space. Unless they're sonic death waves, maybe.

The people you pass don't give you strange glances like you expected they would. Most of them are guys who appear to be busy, either carrying something or working on some kind of machine.

But there's gotta be somethin' fishy going on.

Soon you reach the passageway at the back of the hangar. It forks in two directions.

You slow the three-wheeler.

"What do you say, John Luke?" you ask. "Do you feel lucky? Well, do ya, punk?"

If left is the lucky way to go, head to page 57.

If right is the lucky way to go, head to page 99.

DIRTY HARRY

YOU AND JOHN LUKE SPRINT from the bathroom to the small, round room that gives you access to the ship's computer system. Commander Noble pointed out this room when you first boarded the ship, but you never thought you'd need to enter it. Even though the lights are steadily shutting down throughout the spacecraft, the screens in this room are still blinking and pulsing. There's a single chair in the middle.

"You know more about computers than I do," you tell John Luke.

"Not these computers."

"Hey, all you gotta do is shut this thing down."

Both of you are glancing frantically from screen to screen. You don't have the first idea how to do this.

"Hello, Robertson men," CLINT says.

The door behind you closes. You try to open it, but it won't budge.

"Hey, CLINT, come on. We just wanted some alone time."

"Listen, bud, I know what you two are trying to do." CLINT says this in the most awesome, best Clint Eastwood way yet.

"Look, we don't want to harm you," you say. "But now that we're talking, we're just wondering—like, is there an Off button anywhere?"

"I'm not just gonna let you walk out of here."

At that moment, you see a red button. And hey—it's red and it's a button, so why not?

"John Luke," you mutter out of the corner of your mouth, "press that red button. See what it does."

You hear CLINT laugh at you. "Go ahead; make my day."

John Luke obeys you, and immediately smoke drifts into the room from every direction.

"Only fools press the red button," CLINT says.

"What movie is that from?" you ask, feeling strangely groggy.

"It's called *Time to Sleep Forever*. And it's playing right this very moment."

Your eyelids grow heavy and your face feels droopy, and you sure hope this is all a bad dream.

THE END

TICKET TO THE MOON

WOO-EE—that was some bad dream last night. The worst part wasn't the spinning, either, but seeing your tea cup drifting off bye-bye toward the moon. It was more than you could take.

But that was a nightmare, and now you're about to be living a dream. A dream come true. You're primed and ready, sitting in the equipment room, all set for your first mission out to space!

So . . . they say in space no one can hear you scream.

Okay—really? 'Cause something tells you that's not true.

Some kids dream of growing up and becoming an astronaut, of exploring the moon or taking a spacewalk. But you? You've always dreamed of getting out in the middle of dark, star-speckled outer space and screaming as loud as you can. Then seeing if someone else can hear it.

Today you might get that chance. The moment has come: you're preparing to go into orbit. In about two hours.

Hey—the countdown is T-minus two hours. That's what the voice on the intercom just blared out.

You've already put on your space suit. It has all sorts of cool features, including a pocket for your trademark cap.

This is really happening! It's gonna be Ground Control to Major Si.

Windows lining the room show off the glorious spaceship named the *DC Enterprise* pointed toward the heavens. It's a sleek, shiny silver and has the shape of a—well, frankly, you think it looks like a duck beak. It's long and oval and . . . See here, Jack. It's supposed to resemble a duck. It's the *DC Enterprise*, and the *DC* stands for "Duck Commander," of course.

It's called sponsorship. You got M&M's sponsoring NASCAR. You got Arby's sponsoring roast beef sandwiches. So now you got Duck Commander sponsoring tourists in space.

It's expensive blasting out to space! So half of this expedition is funded by yours truly. Well, not *you* specifically, but the business. And funding is needed, especially when the ship is being readied for commercial flights over the next five years.

Look, if Duck Commander can sponsor a NASCAR race (just like M&M's can), why can't they do the same for a race into space?

This is no old-fashioned space shuttle, either. You could fit several space shuttles into the *DC Enterprise*, especially with its multiple decks on top of each other and all its different compartments inside.

You feel some air blasting into your suit while Willie's worried face studies you.

"You ready, Uncle Si?"

"Ready and able and willing," you tell him.

Yeah, even behind the big ole beard you can see your nephew's concern.

Hey, they're just jealous 'cause I'm finally doing something no other Duck Commander's done.

Your family says you sometimes act like you're orbiting Earth, and now you really get the chance to do it!

You head into the room where astronauts go before they actually shoot up into space. These official guys are making sure your gear is in place and seeing if you're gonna wimp out. But there's no wimping out, Jack!

You're gonna be blasted up there like something out of *Moonraker*. You're gonna get to see the dark side of the moon. And who knows? Maybe it'll be brighter there than they say.

"I still can't believe they're letting *you* go into space," Willie says. "Wait—I can't believe *John Luke* is going with you."

John Luke is nearby, already wearing his suit too. Korie is standing next to him, her anxious look matching Willie's.

The officials have allowed only two civilians to be in here with you guys, so naturally they're John

Luke's parents. And since Duck Commander is partially funding this spaceflight, it's only fitting that Willie and Korie are here representing the company as well.

"You're just jealous that we're going up there," you tell Willie.

"They asked me first," he says.

"Hey, you turned it down first."

"Who woulda run Duck Commander while I was gone?"

"Jase can do a good job."

Willie snorts. "Yeah, if you're putting on a circus. I have a business to run."

"Look, man—I'm focusin' here. You see this face? It's called *focusin'*."

Willie shakes his head and walks up to John Luke to check out his suit. "How you feelin', John Luke?"

"Good," he says.

"You look a bit pale. Have you eaten anything since you puked this morning?"

"I'm fine."

You feel a little bloated yourself since eating four of those beignets at the brunch earlier. Guess the cooks figured since you're from Louisiana, they needed to have some New Orleans food, so there the pastries showed up. Talk about cliché. Cliché with beignets! But you had to be nice and sample a couple. And maybe even a couple more.

Everyone talks for a while as a group of engineers and tech

guys come and check you out some more. They make sure your headset is working with its microphone and earphones.

You won't be landing on the moon or heading to Mars—but maybe that's down the road. A crew will be doing the hard work today, and you and John Luke will be along for the ride.

You've already met the crew of seven and know your lives are in good hands with these top-notch men and women. You have a list of names written out on a piece of paper so you don't forget who they are:

- **Mitch Noble.** Commander of the ship. This is his sixth spaceflight (four with space shuttle *Discovery*). Looks like he could be president someday. Has a thin brown beard, the way yours looked twenty years ago. He's an all-American, apple-pie nice guy.
- **Ben Parkhurst.** Pilot. Third spaceflight. He's almost as funny as you and has a joke for everything you say.
- **Jada Long.** Chief engineer. Fourth spaceflight. Very methodical, like a machine.
- **Wade Turney.** Mission specialist. A tiny, silent guy. You haven't spoken much to him.
- **Kim Sampson.** Mission specialist. Looks like a regular, likable lady who just so happens to be an astronaut.
- **Franco Herrer.** Warrant officer. You don't want to mess with this guy. All muscle. A bouncer heading to space.

- **Ashley Jones.** Science officer. A charming, pretty blonde who'd fit right alongside all the Robertson ladies.

These are the people you'll be heading to space with.

Soon Willie and Korie are hugging John Luke. Willie hands you your trusty Tupperware tea cup.

"You can't leave without this," Willie says.

"Got that right."

"Just bring John Luke back home in one piece, okay?" Willie looks as if he still can't believe he's asking *you* to do this.

"Come on—I went to 'Nam and made it back. Space ain't got nothing on me."

As you and John Luke walk down the hallway to head to the van that goes to the launchpad, you start singing a song. "'Fly me to the moon, and let me shake among the stars.'"

"I think it's 'play among the stars,'" John Luke tells you.

"Well, I'm gonna be shakin' and playin'."

The astro van drives you to the massive *DC Enterprise*, which is strapped onto three blisteringly big rocket launchers. This is like something you might have built when you were a kid, something two feet tall that wouldn't go three feet off the ground without exploding.

I'll keep that little story to myself.

Soon you and John Luke are going up the elevator and walking into the spaceship. The astronauts are already seated and busy in their designated areas. Maybe they're really working on their computer consoles. Maybe they're playing Candy Crush. Who can tell for sure? All you know is the hatch closes behind you, and there's really no going back now.

You can't choose to get off this sucker.

"Space, here we come," you call out to John Luke.

You proceed down a corridor leading to the back, where you two will be seated. It's far away from the bridge, where the commander and the pilot will be. Below you, in the lower level, are the sleeping quarters and maintenance rooms.

You give John Luke the thumbs-up signal.

Soon everything is shaking and you can feel the blasters beneath the ship swaying, and then you feel throttled alive as you boom out to the great beyond.

You quickly pray that you'll both be safe and will make it back home.

Want to play it safe? Do things go smoothly during takeoff? Go to page 75.

Want to live life on the edge? Do things suddenly get rough and dangerous? Go to page 13.

MAN DOWN

A WILD JACKALOPE may be on the loose, but your first priority has to be making sure Wade is okay. You try warning the others through your microphone, but communication doesn't seem to be going through from this part of the ship. Wade's moaning and mumbling about being speared with little antlers and then bitten. His face looks kind of . . . messy.

"Man, this ain't nothin'," you tell him, trying to offer some encouragement. "I saw worse things in 'Nam."

"Did you ever see someone attacked by a killer baby jackalope?" Wade shouts.

"Nah. You got me on that one."

You help him up and try to find something to wipe his face with. There's some kind of garment or blanket in the corner that you give to him.

"Hey, the good news is that you can breathe in this spaceship even though your helmet's destroyed," you tell him.

"Get me out of here!"

"We take you outside, you're gonna die," you tell him. "We gotta get you another helmet. Maybe a rabies shot too."

He doesn't find that very funny.

You try the microphone again. "Commander Noble, you guys copy? Anybody out there? SOS? Hello, is there anybody *out there*?"

Nothing.

Wade's beginning to get loopy. "I'm gonna die! I'm gonna die out here, bit by a bunny!"

"Nobody's dying, okay, Jack? Got it? Come on. What's that Journey song? 'Don't stop believin'! Hold on to that feelin'! Duh-duh, duh-duh . . . small-town boy . . .'" That's all you got.

Wade's shaking his head, delirious, appearing seriously cuckoo for Cocoa Puffs. "That's it, man. Game over, man, game over! What are we gonna do now? What are we gonna do?"

You're singing Journey, trying to calm him, but it's not working.

"If you don't stop singing, I'm gonna explode," he shouts.

"Easy, killer."

Yes, Wade's definitely turning aggressive and crazy.

"Come on—let's get to the entryway. I'll help you." You pull Wade up and drag him toward the ship's exit but sit him in a corner before you get too close to the door. "Stay here for now. I'm going to step outside, try to phone the others. We need to figure how you're supposed to breathe out there."

For a moment after you step through the door, you expect to see the jackalope. Or maybe his family and friends. But you don't see anything except a dark, barren moonscape.

"Commander Noble? John Luke? You guys copy?"

Good thing for you—and *really* good thing for Wade—they do copy.

• • •

An hour later, you get back to the *DC Enterprise*. John Luke and Commander Noble came to retrieve you, bringing Wade a special space suit designed for the wounded. The three of you help him into the *Enterprise*. You haven't had time to explain what happened to him because you don't really *know* what happened! You're wondering if it's all in your mind. But Wade is clearly wounded, so nope. Not all in your mind.

Once you're back on the ship, Wade is taken to the infirmary and treated by Ashley Jones, the science officer. You take off your space suit and join the rest of the crew to debrief.

"It was a small alien life-form that attacked him," you tell the crew.

"What kind of alien life-form?" Ben Parkhurst asks.

Well, uh, you see . . . Um, the truth is . . .

"Far out there," you answer. "Like, *really* far out."

Lots of questions come your way, so many that you can't

answer them all at once. No, you didn't find any other living things on the ship, just skeletons. Yes, the alien seemed violent (and cuddly!). No, you didn't get bitten. Yes, the alien got away (and you think it was hopping!).

"So, Silas," Commander Noble eventually says, "what are we dealing with here? The truth. You've been saying a lot of nothing. Just tell us."

Do you tell them the truth? Go to page 171.

Do you describe the jackalope in a vague, safe way? Go to page 219.

TAKE ME WITH U

"**HEY, JACK,** if there's someone in trouble, then help is my middle name," you say.

Everybody looks at you like they're confused.

"I think he's meaning to say *providing* help is his middle name," John Luke says.

"That's right. I got the red cape on and the blue tights."

"Sounds sort of scary," Commander Noble says.

"Si in tights," Pilot Parkhurst laughs. "Yes. The world isn't ready."

"Universe," you say. "We're talking universe."

"Ben, what's our best option here?" Noble says.

"Can I parachute?" you ask.

Nobody thinks that's funny. You win some and you lose some.

"Sir, we haven't tested it," Parkhurst says, "but the ship has the capability to perform a horizontal drop and removal. It's essentially the same as a landing, just a little quicker."

The crew waits and watches to see what the commander will say. Franco eats his cereal, Ashley looks over the reports in her hands, and Commander Noble stands and stares at you.

"I approve of this decision," he finally concedes. "But I have to tell all of you—the lives of everybody on this ship may be endangered if we head to that moon."

"And we might be leaving some stranded souls behind on some weird moon if we don't see what's happening," you remind him. Wasn't he the one who wanted to respond to the signal in the first place?

"Agreed," Noble says. "But, Silas—I need you to come out into the unknown with me."

"Man, I've been dealin' with the unknown ever since I first started working at Duck Commander."

"We'll give it an hour," the commander announces. "Then I want everyone suited up and ready to go."

• • •

Shortly before the descent begins, John Luke asks if you're sure about this.

"We don't know who's making that distress signal. Couldn't it be an alien?"

"Jep could be an alien too," you say. "You just don't know with anybody these days. Humanoids and thyroids and all kinds of 'roids."

"I think you mean androids, not thyroids," John Luke says.

"Yep, those too!"

"Then I'll come outside with you."

"Nope. You stay in here. Gotta respect your parents' wishes."

"What if something happens to you?"

You take a sip of iced tea from your cup. Being the sponsor means they have unsweetened tea on board. All you can drink. But you can't bring it to Phobos with you.

"Use the focus, John Luke."

"You mean force?"

"No, I mean focus. You don't want the dark sight."

John Luke shakes his head. You wonder what it is you said.

The landing only takes about ten minutes, but it seems to go on forever. The shaking and motion feel different. As they should, maybe. It's amazing that a massive machine like the *DC Enterprise* can also be handled and flown like some small twin-engine plane.

When Commander Noble gives the okay, you and John Luke unbuckle and head to the entrance/exit lift.

"I want to go with you guys," John Luke says again.

You give Noble a look. He shakes his head as if it's not a good idea.

"What's it look like out there?" you ask.

"Mostly rock," Ashley Jones says. "Subzero temperatures. Dangerous. Very difficult to sustain life outside."

"But you got an SOS, right?"

"Yes. And signs of life. The gang back home will be *very* interested to see what we find."

"I'll stay right with you guys," John Luke says. "I promise."

Do you let John Luke come with you?
Go to page 143.

Do you make John Luke stay behind in the spaceship? **Go to page 161.**

THAT VOICE AGAIN

LISTEN, JACK. Waitin's usually for wussies, but sometimes you gotta be smart. Or sometimes you gotta pretend to be smart, at least. So for now, you wait in the hallway right next to the spaceship hangar, just like you were told. You can hear people banging on the door that Commander Noble programmed. They're even taking some shots at it.

You're watching the commander to see if you can tell when he wants you to go over to the *DC Enterprise*. But then two things happen.

Two not-so-good things.

Hey, when it rains, it pours, even in the dark armpits of outer space.

First, the *DC Enterprise* explodes! Or at least a portion of it does.

"Aw, man, I liked that ship!" you say. Then you wonder if

anyone was nearby or still on it. *Oh no—Commander Noble! Is he okay?*

You turn and see the gold helmet of Mr. D. walking toward you.

"How'd you get here?" you ask.

He's holding something in his hands. It's a sword.

You hear his heavy breathing.

Hang on a minute.

"I've been waiting for you, Silas," he says.

The voice sounds different from before.

Then you hear—

Is he laughing?

"The circle is now complete." D. continues to approach with the sword.

You don't see any circles.

"You're weak, old man," D. says as he breathes heavily.

Like he's just trying to sound ridiculous.

You stand your ground, holding up your fists. Suddenly a voice calls from the hangar.

"Uncle Si!"

It's John Luke.

You look through the window at John Luke and wonder if you'll have to sacrifice yourself . . .

Hold on, Jack. I'm not sacrificing anything! I'm running like a squirrel.

Then D. does something crazy.

He takes off his helmet.

It's Jase. Your nephew. Your crazy, cuckoo nephew. Unless they've cloned him.

"Man, you got the funniest look on your face, Si."

"Hey—you were about to be attacked."

"Funny, 'cause I'm holding the sword. Couldn't find a lightsaber on this ship."

You point through the window at John Luke, and Jase quickly pulls him through the door Commander Noble used.

"How'd you get here?" John Luke asks.

"Long story," Jase says. "Well, actually, it's pretty short, to be honest."

You hear pounding on the door. "Okay, tell us later. We can act out childhood movies on your own time, Jack. Let's get out of here."

"Hold on, hold on," Jase says. "Not that way."

"Where are we going?"

"I'll show you. Come with me."

Go to page 247.

ROLLING IN THE DEEP

YOU START PUSHING BUTTONS, hoping to find the right combination to get this ship moving. John Luke hits some too and manages to engage the cyclone thrusters.

The good news is you figure out how to steer the ship into open space. And yeah, you really *can* steer this ship.

The bad news is this part of space isn't so open after all. You steer the ship straight into an asteroid field.

"Uh, Uncle Si?" John Luke asks.

"Houston, we have a problem. A big problem."

These asteroids sure are big. And rolling around in all sorts of ways. Makes your brain a bit dizzy, Jack.

But, hey—you've played the video games before. You've seen the movies. It's not that difficult to avoid getting hit by—

GAME OVER

DOWN THE LINE

YOU DECIDE TO GO LEFT, so you ditch the three-wheeler and head down the hallway for a few minutes before reaching another intersection. Your hallway connects with a larger one, and this new passage has lots of people walking in it. And the weirdest thing is that they all look . . .

Normal. Like the men working in the hangar, but even more normal than that.

You see a man in a business suit carrying a briefcase. Another man right behind him wearing khaki pants and a button-down shirt. You pass a woman dressed in a hat and uniform, who appears to work at some kind of fast-food chain. There's a girl in sparkly jeans and the kind of tennis shoes that light up.

It's sorta the way malls used to be when they were actually full of people. Or maybe even more than that, it's the way a big-city sidewalk looks.

A woman passes who looks like a librarian. A mechanic guy passes next, dressed in a grease-stained T-shirt and jeans.

"What is this?" John Luke whispers.

"Something weird's going on. I know that."

"I feel like we're back home and not on a spaceship."

You nod. For a few minutes you continue walking in silence. Just passing by normal people.

You pull John Luke aside so nobody can hear you.

"Here's my thinking," you begin. "These are all androids that are supposed to look like people. Or maybe they're aliens wearing human costumes."

"Those would be some good costumes."

"Or they're cones."

"Cones?" John Luke asks. "I think you mean clones."

"No, I think it's cones."

"A cone is like an ice cream cone. A conehead."

"Well, whatever. Clone, cone. These regular-looking people are anything but."

You realize you're speaking in a very loud whisper, so you look around to make sure nobody's listening.

"So what do we do?"

"I say we pick someone who looks like us and follow them."

"A guy in camo with a big beard and glasses who's walking around with a teenager?"

You think for a minute. "Okay, let's just find another teen boy. Clean-cut. Good-looking like you. Likable."

"And what?"

"Follow him."

That's exactly what you end up doing. The boy you see is wearing jeans and a New Orleans Saints jersey, so he has to be a good guy, right? He's from New Orleans. He's practically family.

Which may be exactly what they want you to think right before they decide to *eat you* . . . well, right before something happens. You and John Luke just need to find out what that something will be.

The teenager walks by himself in a crowd full of these regular-looking people heading toward an elevator while the two of you follow a dozen yards behind. He puts a hand up to push a white square panel on the wall, and a door slides open to his left.

You stop and pull John Luke back.

"Shouldn't we go in?" he asks.

A part of you says no. Another part says yes. And another part wonders how Rocky beat Mr. T in *Rocky III*. Because, really, there's no way that could have happened.

"I pity the fool."

"Uncle Si?"

"Maybe we should split up."

Do you both go inside? Go to page 183.

Do you tell John Luke to go inside alone, while you take the elevator to another floor to look for the crew? Go to page 89.

END OF THE LINE

"I DON'T THINK GOING BACK out there's gonna help us any," you tell John Luke.

You realize this room has started glowing.

Suddenly you feel a bit light-headed. Sorta strange. Hey—you've been a little off ever since coming to space, but now you're feeling really wacky.

"You feel that, John Luke?"

"Yeah. Kinda seems like I'm floating."

"Well, we *are* in space, you know."

"Yeah. But this is different."

The door opens.

"Quick, let's go!" you tell John Luke.

But as you start to run, something happens to you.

You find yourself in the driver's seat of a car. Wait, Jack—a hologram of a car, not a real one. It's half-there and half-not.

You're no longer running. Now you're racing.

"John Luke?"

He blows by you in a Jeep. A 3-D hologram-like Jeep.

"Look at this, Uncle Si!" he shouts. "I think we just morphed into a video game."

You're moving at breathtaking speed on some kind of grid. You try to keep up with John Luke but can't.

Then you turn around and see more glowing cars following you.

You wonder if the others can hear the awesome techno music accompanying this race.

A nice little drive in the middle of the 3-D video game funky dunky solar system.

That's a fact, Jack.

You ride around for a few minutes, sending the chasing cars in circles and causing some of them to crash and explode. But they blow up just like something might in a video game or a book that has twenty-some endings. You don't take it to heart.

"I see an exit, Uncle Si!"

You keep leaning forward. That's what's propelling this game.

John Luke's glowing Jeep Wrangler takes a jump and goes flying.

"You okay, John Luke?"

He's hooting and hollering.

Soon you've evaded all the cars following you.

The song is coming to an end.

The Exit sign is approaching.

You aim your car straight at it and then . . .

You're out.

You're floating, flying, rushing—hey, wait a minute. Now you're falling, fumbling, tumbling, turning over and over.

Then your head hits something and you black out.

• • •

When you wake up, you call out for John Luke, but he's nowhere to be found. You're in a large, empty warehouse, and it's glowing, but not blue like the racing room—more like a metallic gray. You notice several doors along the walls.

"Hello?" you call out. "Anybody there? Hello? Is it me you're looking for?"

But nobody's looking for you, Jack.

When you open the first door and peer in, you get this weird sensation inside. 'Cause you hear a familiar sound—a *waka-waka-waka-waka*. Reminds you of Pac-Man. So you shut *that* door.

Feeling braver, you open the second door, and now you're on a street covered with massive dudes fighting. You get out of there.

By the third door, when Donkey Kong starts chasing you, you realize you're stuck in some kind of arcade game nightmare and you can't get out.

John Luke must've escaped, but as for you? Well, it's game *never* over for you, Jack.

You're gonna have to blast asteroids and defeat space invaders and try to slay the dragon in its lair.

You're not sure how this happened or how you got here, but you're pretty sure it's gonna take you a *lot* longer to get out of this.

If you can get out.

High Score: 0000000000000000

THE END

WRONG

YOU RAISE YOUR HAND. Curiosity may have killed the cat, but it never did you any harm. "So, hey, Jack, I'm just wondering—refresh this ole head of mine, will you? What's the mission again?"

The teacher's eyes come to life. He looks at you and nods. "Yeah, yeah, sure thing."

The others are all looking at you too.

"Something I said? The man asked if we had questions."

The teacher turns and presses something in the wall, then faces you again. "The mission. The great mission. Anybody want to tell our new friend here what the mission might be?"

"Infiltration," one voice says.

"Assimilation," another says.

"Disintegration," a third person says. It's the guy with the ponytail who answered the door when you knocked.

"Well, that sounds dandy," you say. "Can I add indigestion to that? 'Cause, man, I ate these pickled eggs, and woo-ee."

Nobody laughs. Nobody even smiles.

Then the door opens and three men walk in. They all look like pirates. You can't help but let out a laugh as they approach you.

"Ahoy, me mateys!" you say.

They gather in front of you. The one you'd call Blackbeard—since he's got a long, braided black beard and the fluffiest of hats—smiles back at you.

Then he cracks his elbow over your skull, and like that, it's lights out, Jack.

Go to page 169.

SAFETY DANCE

SO YOU MADE IT. You're here. You've arrived.

You're in a safe place. No free-fallin' here, Jack, 'cause hey—you've landed.

Did you bring your friends? And do they dance? Because if they don't dance . . .

We can dance. And sing.

Hey—nobody *made* you come here. This is dance hall days, baby! Come on, Jack. Get out on the dance floor.

Confused?

Maybe the lack of oxygen is making you hear strange sounds.

Maybe this is the most brilliant piece of prose and you have no idea what the meaning is behind it.

A black duck call entity in the deepest reaches of space?

What does it symbolize?

Two helmet-wearing danger lords ruling the darkest spaces out of reach?

Whom do they stand for?

And the jackalope?

Look behind the clues. The truth is out there.

Huh?

Seek, and ye shall find, Silas.

Wait, what?

Maybe you need more answers in this life. If so, then open the Bible, Jack.

Maybe you need more fun in your life. Then pour yourself a glass of tea and do what you do best.

Dance . . .

THE END

Or is it the beginning? Turn to page 1.

HUNGRY LIKE THE WOLF

BOTH YOU AND JOHN LUKE decide to peer into the door slot. You see two figures with their backs toward you. They're talking, but you can't understand them. Their language is unfamiliar and sounds like some kind of animal howling. You start to say something, but John Luke puts up a hand and says, "Shhhh!"

Then he motions for you to watch.

From the back, they appear to be ordinary men. They're wearing black outfits. You see a couple of helmets on a table nearby. One is silver and the other is gold.

"Mr. Mister?" you whisper to John Luke.

"The misters," he whispers back.

"Any difference?"

"Shh."

One of the men walks over to the side of the room you

can't see. Then he comes into view again, and you see his face for the first time.

"What's wrong with that dude?" John Luke whispers, jumping back from the horrifying sight.

"I don't think that's a dude. Guy must be an alien lizard in disguise or something."

That said, you both start sprinting down the stairs. You can't get away fast enough.

Who knew that space could be this terrifying.

Go to page 125.

DANGER ZONE

MISSION SPECIALIST WADE TURNEY heads down the slope with you to investigate the spacecraft. One thing you can't help wondering is what Wade's "specialty" happens to be. Why don't they call you a mission specialist too? Can he do magic tricks or speak like a ventriloquist? Like, seriously—you want to know his special feature.

But you're mainly just relieved you were able to keep John Luke from volunteering. It was touch and go for a while, but you finally convinced him by promising he could come along on the next scary, uncertain mission.

It doesn't look like this spaceship's been active for years. There's a coating of grime and dirt on it. You and Wade examine the surface, trying to find a door in.

"Hey, you think the door is in the part that's sunk into the ground?" you ask Wade.

"I'm not sure," he says.

Some specialist you are. I give your specialty level a D minus, Jack.

You think the back of the spacecraft is what's protruding from the ground, as if the ship crashed straight into the surface. But it didn't explode. That's the crazy thing. It resembles a dart stuck into a board.

"I found something." Wade gestures to a panel on the ship's side.

"You guys okay down there?" Commander Noble asks.

A doorway slides open.

"Yes, sir," Wade says. "Think we just located an entryway."

"Be careful."

"Wish I had a gun," you mutter.

It always feels better having a defense mechanism in your hands when you're entering a strange, alien-like spaceship stranded on some lifeless moon full of odd-looking antlers.

Forget the Duckmen—you need the Buckmen.

Wade points his powerful flashlight into the open doorway. Then he steps inside.

"What do you see?" Commander Noble asks right away.

"Nothing yet."

You follow him in. You'd be feeling okay, except your space diaper is causing a bit of a wedgie, and it's starting to really annoy you. But other than that, you're doing great.

Of course, the skeletons you encounter on the ship don't

really settle so well with your stomach. In one room, you find two of them sitting at a table as if they're involved in the longest game of chess *ever*. You expect to find cobwebs or something around here, but yeah, this ain't no haunted house. Haunted spacecrafts on Martian moons don't get cobwebs. Just bones.

"Think those were humans?" you ask Wade.

"Check out that head. Does *that* look human?"

You squint closely at it. "Actually, no. That thing kinda looks like a jack-o'-lantern."

"The skeletal remains of one."

You both enter a room with several tables and chairs, like some kind of kitchen or dining area. No skeletons can be seen in here. Closed doors lead off in two different directions.

"How's it look down there?" Commander Noble asks. "Does it appear to be dangerous?"

"'Right into the Danger Zone,'" you start to sing.

"Oh, boy," Wade sighs.

"You sound just like Willie."

"I should be with you. Let me come down!" John Luke shouts over the radio.

"You stay there. We've got this," you fire back, hoping you can keep him from striking out on his own.

"We discovered what are almost certainly the remains of a couple life-forms down here," Wade reports. "Still checking out the ship."

"So what do you say, Jack?" you ask him. "Which door?"

Wade shrugs. "You sound eager to choose. Go ahead."

You shine your flashlight at one door and notice some markings on it. They look like scratches. Like some rabid animal was tearing at the door, trying to get in. Or maybe it was trying to escape. Or maybe it was just a lady with long fingernails who really wanted to leave this party?

The other door doesn't have the markings on it.

"It's probably smarter to open that door first, right?" You point to the door without the markings on it.

But maybe that's what they *want* you to think.

Do you open the door without the scratches on it?
Go to page 135.

Do you open the door with the scratches on it?
Go to page 81.

COUNTING STARS

SMALL WINDOWS line each side of where you and John Luke are sitting, and through them you see the fading, falling world outside. For a while all you can do is look ahead and try not to think of that crawfish boil you had last night. You eventually feel the blasters stop and rip away from the ship, and then things calm down. You glance to the round window and see nothing but darkness. But soon something else comes into view.

Something that stops your breathing it's so beautiful.

"Look at that," you say over your headset. It's your home planet . . . but so quiet and still, it feels impossible that you actually live there.

"It's amazing," John Luke says. "Wish I could take a picture."

"Take the picture in your head. Snap. There it goes. Just like that. Better than a Polaroid."

Commander Noble is talking a lot, and there's back-and-forth with Pilot Parkhurst and Mission Control that you can hear on your earbuds.

"You two doing okay back there?" Commander Noble asks.

"We're ready to start floating," you say.

For the next half hour, it seems like things are going smooth and steady. Until Commander Noble tells Mission Control that he's spotting something strange. Then he sends you an interpersonal message only you can hear on your radio headset.

"Silas," he says, "we have a little situation."

"'Move out—don't mess around,'" you sing back.

"What?"

"Never mind. What's wrong?"

"It looks like we're not the only ones out here," the commander says. "There's another ship—a massive one—and it's closing in on us."

"A UFO? Classic!"

"I'm not sure I'd call it that. Mission Control isn't finding it on their monitors."

"I've told people there are aliens ever since I was a little boy," you say.

"Well, here's the concern—the *DC Enterprise* is shutting down on us. We could wait to see what the other ship is doing, or we could head to the space station for repairs."

He's asking you! Hey, Jack—sponsorship is pretty cool. You finally have a say.

Maybe you'll ask for some steak and lobster and—

"Silas?"

Do you stay out here and see what the other ship is all about? Go to page 7.

Do you travel to the nearest space station to make repairs? Go to page 223.

LONELY PLANET

OKAY. SO YOU DO AS YOU'RE TOLD. You wait until the crew is all sleeping, including the science officer; then you get to work. After a few days, you devise a way to tow the escape pod with an unconscious Wade inside. Hey, you're a Robertson. You know how to figure these things out.

But you've missed your opportunity for cybersleep. So you're left to stay awake for the whole trip.

You and your thoughts.

Oh, boy.

You can feel the isolation pressing in. But you've been all around the world. You've known lonely days and lonely nights. It's okay. You can take the long way home.

Inside your head, you've got enough songs to blow up an iPhone. You can sing them to yourself and hum them in your imagination.

You can see the stars blinking.

You can pretend you're part of the scenery.

They're probably talking about this big trip on the news right now. Ole Uncle Si. Silly Uncle Si saving the day.

When you come back, they'll throw a ticker-tape parade. And they rarely have those kinds of things these days.

You're bringing the ticker tape back, Jack.

You settle in for a long ride. Coasting. Snoozing. Snacking. And sipping your iced tea.

It's a tough job, but someone's gotta save the universe. And hey, if they need you again, you'll be ready.

But not until you get back down to see your family and have some down-home food only a woman from Louisiana seems to have mastered.

You are *hungry*.

But you're safe and sound, and that's what matters.

Soon you're floating and falling and flying for a little bit. It's a sweet sort of thing.

After an awesome, amazing journey like this, all you can do is smile and thank the good Lord for safe travels home.

The familiar sight of Earth comes into view after a while. You're floating far above it—and you think you might be able to see West Monroe, way down there.

Eventually you land back on Earth and get your two legs underneath you. It's kinda hard to walk at first, but soon it'll be time to start moving and shaking again.

THE END

TINY DANCER

YOU OPEN THE DOOR with the scratches and discover a room that's in total disarray. It looks like the interior of some kind of cabin, but the beds are turned over and the drawers are on their sides. All sorts of things are on the floor—clothing, papers, some pictures. You don't see anybody, however.

"I don't think the crash caused this," you tell Wade, who's behind you.

Both of you are shining your lights all around the room since darkness still smothers the entire ship.

You can hear Wade's heavy breathing behind you.

"Si! You see that?"

Wade's light is pointing up toward the corner of the room. That's when you spot it.

You shuffle back a bit, freaked out at what you're witnessing.

"That thing real?" Wade asks.

You've heard about creatures like this before, but never in a million years did you think you'd actually see one in person.

"Yeah, Jack, I think so," you say.

It doesn't move but just sits there, so silent and peaceful and cute.

"That's like the most adorable thing I've ever seen," Wade says, starting to move toward it.

You grab him and throw him back against the wall. "Hey, Jack, listen to me. That there is the most terrifying creature in existence. You need to stay away from it."

Wade laughs. "How can that be? You seeing the same thing I'm seeing?"

Both of your lights shine on the creature, which sits on a small ledge slightly above head level. It resembles a baby rabbit, a cute little light-brown bunny. Except . . .

Oh, the horror of it all . . .

It has tiny antlers.

Just like the kind you walked past outside. Except the ones outside were massive.

Mama and papa and grandpa and grandma . . .

"Come on. It's so sweet," Wade says, but you restrain him with an arm so he can't move farther.

"That's how they catch you off guard."

You've heard rumors about creatures like this.

"How *what* catches you off guard?" Wade asks.

"That's a jackalope. I've only heard about them. But now I'm seein' one. With my own four eyes."

"A jackalope?" Wade starts to laugh.

"Don't laugh. It knows when you're mocking it."

Wade only cracks up more. "The little thing is probably afraid of us."

"Look here—that 'little thing' probably destroyed this room. Maybe it took down the whole spaceship!"

But Wade doesn't want to hear it. He moves past you and shoves a chair out of his way to get to the small creature.

"I'm tellin' you," you say.

"You're crazy."

The creature gazes straight ahead with tiny eyes that could haunt a man's darkest nightmares. So innocent and so precious on the outside . . .

And so dreadful with their evil intentions on the inside.

Wade is right underneath its ledge now, and he pulls over a chair to stand on so he can pick up the animal.

The jackalope has other plans.

It jumps.

No—it doesn't just jump. The thing launches into Wade. It lands on his helmet, crushing it with its tiny paws.

He begins screaming even as you rush to help him.

"Get it off me! Get it off me—get it off!"

You finally grab it and rip it away.

"Where is it? Get it! Now!"

You know you have to get him away from here.

Go to page 43.

BETWEEN STARS

AS IF THERE WERE *ANY* WAY you'd say no to Mars. Come on now.

You and John Luke set up a video conference call with the family back home in West Monroe. They all want to know how things are going and how you're feeling and what it's like to use the bathroom in outer space. You know—the really important things.

Then you're suddenly preparing for Mars and forced to go to meetings and study reports, and hey, this ain't high school or college days again! You just want to hop in the spaceship and strap yourself in and get ready to go.

Still, it's supposed to take 124 days to get to Mars.

So let's see—you need to plan a complete schedule of television viewing on your iPad since you have, well, four months.

Maybe you can rewatch *Lost* and try to make sense of . . . Nah, it's still not gonna make sense.

You start thinking of books you want to read and maybe even some more that you could write. But then Commander Noble informs you and John Luke that you won't have to occupy yourselves for four months on the way to Mars.

"Here's another fact we can tell you about now," he says.

"You've invented a way to hunt in space," you say.

"Uh . . . no. But the *DC Enterprise* does have something special it can do. Actually, the space suits are the things that do it."

"Are we able to watch movies through our helmets?" John Luke asks.

"Well, no, but that would be cool," Commander Noble says. "Have you ever heard of a thing called stasis?"

"No, but it sounds a little like steak and biscuits," you say. You can't help it. You're hungry, and this squeezable food they keep giving you is really doing nothing for you. But you've got your tea, so you're getting by, at least.

"It's basically being in a prolonged state of motionlessness," he says.

"I think Willie's in perpetual stasis," you joke.

"Our space suits can induce this condition, a sort of cybersleep, which basically allows our bodies to shut down for long periods of time. So four months will seem like four hours."

"It'll be like time travel," you say.

"No, that's another story," John Luke replies.

"What'd you say?"

But he doesn't answer.

"Departure is less than six hours away," Commander Noble informs you. He leads the two of you to a small waiting room and leaves to take care of preparations.

"You ever think God did all this just to show off?" you ask John Luke as you stare out the room's one window into the infinite beyond. "I mean, just look at it."

"It's amazing," John Luke says, gazing in awe like you.

"I was thinking—it's not enough he made the heavens and the stars. God was like, 'Here we go, and I'm going to do it right.' He decided, 'Let's keep going.' Then he made a thousand-something animals *and* man. I mean, I would've been tuckered out after making the solar systems. I would've said, 'It's Sunday *now*, Jack.'"

"You think we'll ever get back down to Earth?" John Luke asks.

"Of course we will," you tell him. "Hey, I promised your parents. I mean, if somethin' happened to you, Willie'd fly out to space himself to track you down. You have to at least make it long enough to find a pretty lady and get married and have some babies. Forget outer space! Wait until *that* happens. You'll be circling the solar system dealing with a woman."

Soon you're in the *DC Enterprise* again, but this time the flight goes off with barely a motion. You're already in space, so it's not like you need some big takeoff out here.

Before cybersleep comes, the commander's voice speaks in your helmet once more.

"Okay, ladies and gentlemen. Time to take our four-month snooze. The space suits will keep your body nice and steady. Make sure you have happy dreams. I'll see you on the other side of Mars."

You picture your family back home, then think of your iced tea, and slowly but surely your eyes drift closed.

Do you have pleasant dreams on your journey?

Go to page 227.

Do you have nightmares on your journey?

Go to page 11.

BEING HUMAN

YOU PRESS THE OPEN BUTTON a bunch of times. This elevator isn't responding the way the ones back home do. Finally the door slides back. You scan the hallway of the thirteenth floor, trying to spot any clues to where the astronauts might be. You pick a direction and start walking when someone stops you.

"Hey, I know you," the man says.

It's a younger man, maybe in his twenties, and he's wearing all camouflage. You've never seen him before.

"I'm sorry, son," you tell him.

"No, you're Si Robertson."

You shake your head, figuring denial is best at this point.

"Yeah, we've seen you on our planet before."

"Hold on, Jack. You've *seen* me?"

"Sure," the guy says. "Oh, we're big supporters of Duck

Commander. We own a little store called Beef Eaters. We've been ordering from you folks ever since Phil started selling his duck calls. In fact, he was one of the first humans we ever met."

"So y'all aren't humans, then." You know that much already, but maybe this guy's about to explain what exactly they are.

The man shakes his head. "No way."

"How'd we ship things to you on another planet?"

"Oh, only the postal service knows. Shh. I can't say anything. A big conspiracy of sorts."

You're peering around to see if anybody else is watching you. "Well, it's been nice to talk."

"Hey, wait, I can't let you go, Si."

"Why not?"

"Uh, 'cause you're *you*. A human."

"So?"

The guy laughs. "Don't you get it?" He glances around to make sure nobody hears what he's about to say. *"We're invading your planet. Tomorrow."*

"I promise I won't tell a soul."

The man produces something from his pocket. It looks like a golf ball. "I hate to do this, but . . ."

He holds up the golf ball, and you watch it turn red, then yellow, then orange.

Then you black out.

Go to page 169.

WE OWN THE SKY

IT'S BEEN EITHER the best sleep of your life or the worst stretch of snoozing imaginable. But that's been up to you, you know? Sometimes you gotta get some positive thinking before getting some positive snoring.

It takes you a while to get going, however. Commander Noble doesn't simply wake you up via your headset. He's standing over you, nudging you awake. You notice he's out of his space suit.

"We've made it safely," he tells you.

John Luke already has his space helmet off and looks like he's been in a dryer for about an hour.

"How long have you been awake?" you ask the commander.

"A few days. I had to make sure everything was set as we neared the planet."

"Is it still red?"

Noble smiles. "Yes, Si, Mars is still red."

"Shoot. I always thought it was some big illusion or something like that."

"Well, if you want to know the truth . . ."

"People from Earth settled down on it back in the seventies?"

"No. But as for the color—the soil on Mars has a lot of iron oxide in it. It's more like a rust shade."

"Or maybe vampires live there." John Luke laughs with a groggy voice.

"You need to wake up over there, kid," Noble says. "Look—get out of your suits. The oxygen and stabilizers are all calibrated to this planet."

"Did you find the 'entity' from wacky world?" you ask.

"We found . . . something. You'll see. Soon."

• • •

When you convene in the galley an hour later, you get the feeling that all the crew members have been awake longer than you and John Luke. So you ask, and sure enough, it turns out each of them woke up at a different time.

After everyone's gotten some food and liquid in their bellies, the commander starts to explain the plan, Dan.

Just hop on the bus, Gus.

"The first imperative action is to board the *Starsailor* and see if anybody is alive," Noble says. "So far we've been unsuccessful in every attempt at making contact. So we're sending a group to go on board and check things out."

"That sounds good," you say.

"That's what we do, Si," Franco says. He slaps you on the back, and you think you might never breathe again.

"You should know that another group will be heading down to Mars to inspect the entity," Noble points out. "We managed to take some pictures of it after discovering its location. And . . . well, you have to see it for yourself."

Mission Specialist Kim Sampson gives everybody a printout picture of the mysterious thing that brought you to Mars. You look at it and burst out laughing.

"Ha-ha, I get it. Duck Commander and duck calls."

"That's no joke," Commander Noble says. "It's real. We had to look and even do some double takes."

"That's a duck call," you insist, jabbing a finger at the image that appears to have been Photoshopped onto the page.

"It resembles one, but that is no duck call. It's approximately twenty feet tall."

"This thing?" you ask. "It looks like one we make. The Mach 3. All black."

"It's giving off frequencies," Noble says. "The unaided human ear cannot pick them up, but Kim's altered them so we can get a sense of what they're like. Kim, play the recorded transmissions."

The mission specialist takes out her iPad

and begins tapping on it. Soon you hear something that sounds like a wood duck call. Except a *whole lot* creepier.

"That's the worst thing I've ever heard," Ben Parkhurst says. "I think I'll just stay on board here and monitor you guys."

"You're already staying," Noble reminds him.

The noise reminds you of something crying out in distress. Yet the sharp *weeek-weeek-weeek* is so similar to the way Jase might blow a call.

"We need to assign the groups now," Commander Noble says. "Ashley and I are going down to Mars to check out the entity. Wade—" he gestures to the quiet mission specialist, who's sitting near the corner—"will be leading a team over on the *Starsailor*. Ben and Jada will be staying behind on the ship. What will you do, Silas?"

You think about it for a minute. Investigating the duck call sounds really cool. Plus, you're not too sure about this Wade fella. He seems like trouble. This leaves you with only two options. And you're feeling thirsty again.

Do you head down to Mars to investigate this mysterious alien duck call? Go to page 243.

Do you decide to stay on the *Enterprise* with Ben and Jada and drink some tea? Go to page 217.

ROAD TO NOWHERE

YOU BOTH GET OFF THE THREE-WHEELER and head right. Hey—right can't be wrong, can it? You walk down the hallway and pass through several doors that slide open as you approach them.

You find yourself in some sort of shipping area where dozens of people are working. They have weird plastic suits on that are all sorts of different colors. Bright colors. Yellow, orange, red, green, purple, and blue. Their faces are covered by masks.

"Should we head back the way we came in?" John Luke asks.

"No. Let's see what's going on here."

Despite these workers' colorful suits, they all seem to be running a typical assembly line operation. You walk around and soon discover what they're packaging.

It's the same thing you saw pictured in the large bay area you just left behind.

Froot Loops.

This makes no sense. . . .

That's right. The secret to the universe is Froot Loops, folks, and little did you know they were made in outer space.

You see the boxes and everything.

"I don't get it," John Luke says.

"Oh, we're gonna get it."

Some of the workers on the line are individually sorting the Froot Loops. They seem to be examining every one of them.

No, not examining them, but putting something on them.

These inspectors hold tiny tubes in their hands and appear to be attaching something to the individual *red* Froot Loops.

You think about asking someone what's up with the red ones. Why not orange? But abrupt shouting across the room sorta makes you forget the question.

Especially because the voice is yelling, "Intruders! Stop them!"

"Is he talking about us?" John Luke asks.

"Yeah. Run!"

You spot the nearest exit, which is different from the door you came in. You tear through it, making sure John Luke is following you. But he passes you by, and then he seems to realize he can't follow you and run in front of you at the same time. So he slows down, and you plow right into him.

When you get up, you turn and see a group of men approaching you. You start to laugh because they're dressed like pirates. Maybe not the "yo, ho, ho, and a bottle of rum" sort of pirates since this isn't the seven seas nor is it a Disney ride, but still. Pirates.

"Come on, Uncle Si!" John Luke says.

There's a blinking red sign on the doorway you're now approaching. A sign that says *Do Not Go In*.

"Come on, Uncle Si!"

"You just said that!" You're wondering if John Luke is feeling okay. Can he not see the sign?

"Hey, John Luke, I don't think—"

But John Luke opens the door anyway. The door with the sign that says *Do Not Go In*. Then he enters and disappears with a loud squeal.

Did he just fall?

You stop for a minute and contemplate whether you should follow. Until you see a six-inch dagger soar by your ear and stick in the wall next to you.

Okay, I'm going in.

When you walk through the doorway, two things happen simultaneously.

You feel yourself falling.

And you smell something really, truly dreadful.

Then you land in a pile of mushy mush.

And for a moment you black out. But not because you're sixty-six years old and fleeing for your life through space.

It might be because you just flung yourself into some kind of Dumpster on a spaceship and you landed on a giant metal something-or-other.

• • •

At some point you wake up again.

"Uncle Si?"

It's John Luke, standing over you.

"Where are we?" you mutter.

"I shut the door. The problem is . . . I shut all of them."

You have the worst headache ever.

"Were those pirates following us?" you ask.

John Luke nods.

"Are we currently in a smelly trash heap?"

He nods again.

"Well, it could be worse."

Then you hear something awful. Something unspeakable. Something dreadful.

And it's right beneath you!

"Something seems to be alive in here," John Luke says.

Hmmmmmm.

Do you get your pocketknife out and try to deal with the thing underneath you? Go to page 127.

Do you try to open the doors to the room you're in? Go to page 139.

LIVE AND LET DIE

AS THE NIGHTMARE SHOCK WAVES of the alien duck call continue to go off, with all of your comrades now on the ground writhing in pain, you decide to do something.

The only thing you can do.

You switch your radio to the broadcast setting, and you start to sing.

"'Who let the dogs out—*woof, woof, woof, woof*,'" you belt out.

Hey, it's not much. But it's the only thing you can think of.

"'Who let the dogs out,'" you keep singing.

Suddenly the shrieking duck call stops. It actually stops, Jack!

Everybody stands up again, breathless and dazed and trying to recover.

John Luke speaks first. "What happened?"

"I don't know," you say.

"Why'd it just stop?" Commander Noble asks.

"I was just—I started to sing, but—"

The shrilling duck call sounds again in all its awful terror. So you quickly resume singing.

"'Live and let die . . . ,'" you sing, then realize you don't know the lyrics. So you just start humming and making sounds to the music.

The duck call stops.

"Keep singing," John Luke says. "Go, Uncle Si!"

"Give me a song," you say. "Fast! Anybody."

"'Happy,'" John Luke suggests.

"'Jump' by Van Halen," Commander Noble says.

"'We Are Never Ever Getting Back Together,'" Ashley Jones adds.

Everyone looks at her with glances that say, *Really?*

You decide to go ahead and pick your own song.

"'You should be dancing, yeah; you should be dancing!'"

The giant floating duck call does the unexpected. It blasts out into space and begins to move erratically through the sky.

"It's doing it! It's dancing," John Luke says. "Kinda like WALL-E."

"Keep singing, Silas!" the commander says.

You start singing whole songs or only their choruses. The problem is, you don't always remember even the whole chorus. Or any of the lyrics. In which case you just make something up.

You might be the first one in the history of man to go from "Ticket to Ride" to "Low Rider" to "Friends in Low Places." Hey, Jack—you can't explain how your mind works.

"'Beat it, beat it,'" you call out while the black thing in the sky swirls and streams back and forth. "'Don't have a heartbeat, so beat it. Tell 'em you're funky; tell 'em you're right. If they don't get you, know you're gonna bite—so beat it.'"

"Uh, Uncle Si," John Luke says over the radio.

"Don't mess with the magic."

You're searching your thoughts for more songs so you can continue as the human jukebox when you see the gliding duck call fly directly into your ship. There's a massive explosion in the sky.

Uhhhhhhhhh . . . "Did that just happen?"

No one answers.

But now the hurtling mass of a machine is coming down from the skies. It's the *DC Enterprise*.

Something pops up and out—it's an escape pod.

Well, at least the other crew members are probably safe.

You stop singing.

The commander is screaming and yelling.

You pull John Luke to the side. "You all right?"

"Yeah. I'm just hoping Ben and Jada are okay."

Lots of voices are crackling over the radio. It sounds like total chaos.

"We have to go to the escape pod for Ben and Jada," Commander Noble says.

Do you join the group heading for the escape pod to check on Ben and Jada? Go to page 131.

Do you decide to start singing again because you really and truly can't believe what you just saw? Go to page 19.

THROW IN THE TOWEL

SOME MIGHT SAY THIS IS GIVING UP. Or giving in. But you'd call it both and then say see ya later and sayonara.

Hey, Jack, sometimes you gotta throw in the towel. Unless you just got out of the shower—'cause in that case, keep the towel till you get some clothes on!

You decide it'll be best to go home now, even if you have to be tucked into some more cybersleep. The crew members keep making arguments like *"Someone might be alive on the planet!"* and *"We owe it to them to examine the distress signal!"* and *"There's danger in being put back to sleep too soon!"*

But you care about priorities, not exclamation points. You know Willie and the boys cannot manage things on their own. Your family needs you. The whole world needs Uncle Si.

Yeah. It's snoozy time for you.

So a few hours later you're all back in your space suits. And

Commander Noble puts in the commands and gets everybody to fall unconscious one by one. This is like Thanksgiving after Miss Kay's cooking when everybody is sprawled around and knocked out cold with bellies full.

You feel good about the decision you made. Your eyes begin shutting, and you assume when you open them again, you'll be able to spot Earth outside the window. . . .

THE END

DON'T STOP

IT'S A GOOD PLAN, taking out the ships. You figure all those vessels you spotted in the hangar must be the ones that are going to attack Earth.

"Mission Control said they couldn't detect the ship we're on," you tell John Luke. "Obviously they have some way of shielding themselves. Like a cloak thing. So you know what we do?"

"What?"

"Make them permanently invisible. And blow them up."

You find what appear to be timer-controlled bombs in the weapons stash. And the strangest thing is that they look like six-packs of Diet Coke.

"I think I understand what they're trying to do," John Luke says. "Everything they're doing—the people, these weapons—they're hiding the truth. Nothing is what it appears to be. A teenager really isn't a teenager. A cowbell—"

"Really isn't a cowbell," you finish for him. "John Luke, you went out in space and got smarter."

"Must be something in the air."

"Let's each take a pack of Diet Coke," you say. "We got some blowing up to do."

Before you're able to get out of the armory, a woman in a pirate outfit walks into the room. You can't help but start to laugh, but then you control it.

"What are you two doing here?" she demands.

Oh, man. You know you can say only a few things. But you're betting only one response will be the right one. Isn't that how it usually goes?

Do you tell her you need these weapons for the mission? Go to page 205.

Do you tell her you've heard reports that some of these weapons aren't working—and that you're trying to fix them? Go to page 119.

COME TOGETHER

FIRST THINGS FIRST: FIND JOHN LUKE.

The astronauts are already captured, and you know they're alive. Right now you need to get John Luke so the two of you can figure out a plan. Hey, two are better than one.

The room you left John Luke in is empty. The teenage boys' briefing must be over too. They will know their assignments and how to infiltrate high schools on Earth. World domination. They might even plant brain-zapping software in smartphones that will make everyone dumb so the aliens can be in complete control!

Wait, maybe they've already done that!

You start to head down the hallway when you hear someone call your name. It's John Luke.

"Over here," he says, waving from a doorway.

For a second you give him a strange look as you enter the passageway he's standing in.

"John Luke—*why* are you dressed as a pirate?"

He closes the door behind you. "That's what the soldiers are dressed as. Have you seen them?"

"I've seen a few, but I just thought—"

"Yeah, it's kinda crazy. But maybe that's the fashion."

"An army of pirates. Really?"

"Space pirates," John Luke says. "Come on—this is a walkway that leads to an armory. They took us in there after the meeting. It's where I got the outfit. And . . ."

He holds up a triangular object in one hand and takes a drumstick—not the chicken kind—out of his back pocket. After further examination, you realize what John Luke is holding.

"Is that a cowbell?"

"Yes, but . . ."

"This ain't no time for playing games. We got a world to save, Jack."

"I know. Come on."

John Luke rushes down the dimly lit passageway, which forks three ways. He chooses one of the routes, and it ends at a closed door.

"Stand back, Uncle Si," he tells you.

Then he bangs a couple times on the cowbell. It doesn't make any noise.

Instead the door in front of you blasts open. As if two laser beams tore through it.

"Whoa," you say. "What'd you do?"

"This isn't an ordinary cowbell. It's a weapon of some kind."

"It *looks* like a cowbell."

And yeah, you know it, Jack. You can already picture it in your mind. You and John Luke on the battlefield, fighting off aliens, and you've run out of ammo. You call to John Luke, telling him you need more cowbell.

Yep. That's right. A lot of good it will do you then.

John Luke opens the shredded door. He wasn't kidding about the armory.

"There's lots of different kinds of weapons in here," he says. "We were going through the list in our class."

You pull him to the side.

"Hey, you know what we're dealin' with, right?" You decide to speak only in a whisper for the next part. *"These people are planning to invade the US."*

"Not if they can't get off this ship."

"You have a plan?"

"Yeah. The big question is this: do we take out their ships or their leaders?"

Well, look at John Luke, all grown-up and acting like Alexander the Great. Or General Patton.

You think for a minute.

These are good questions from a man holding a magical cowbell in his hand.

Do you take out their ships? Go to page 111.

Do you take out their leaders? Go to page 121.

BRAIN DAMAGE

YOU CHOOSE CYBERSLEEP. How do you know if you can trust that professor guy anyway? Hopefully everything will be better in the morning, like it usually is.

When you first enter cybersleep, you experience a wonderful, familiar sense of security. But a short time later, it feels like you're bouncing around, and you wonder if you're imagining the screams.

Then you wake up and realize you're not.

As soon as you shake off your post-cybersleep confusion, you notice that John Luke is missing. The ship is violently jerking up and down, and you can hear voices down the hallway. After detaching yourself from your seat, you open the door and get a firsthand glimpse of the chaos that awaits you.

The professor or whoever it was—a TV critic, Jack?—happened to be right.

You see an awful, terrible, unspeakable thing—it's John Luke. He's been infected.

Antlers are coming out of his head.

When he sees you, he attacks. And just like that, it's over.

You should've known better.

You should've realized that when you're in space and an alien jackalope gets involved, you don't go on acting like everything's fine and dandy.

Before your transformation, you experience your last thought as Silas Robertson: *I wonder what antlers will look like on my head.*

You bet they'll look pretty cool.

THE END

BRASS MONKEY

"WELL, WE'VE HEARD REPORTS that some of these are not working," you tell the woman.

"Are you sure?" she asks. "You've heard that those bombs in particular don't work?"

You nod.

"That's strange." She touches her wrist, which appears to have some kind of device on it.

Maybe it's one of those smartwatches. Like having an iPhone as a watch. It's the latest technology, and you're really hoping to get one when you're back on Earth.

"Yeah. Strange, Jack," you say, letting *Jack* accidentally slip out of your mouth.

"Want to know the strangest thing about that?" she asks.

You notice her eyes have become dark. Like all black.

That can't be good.

"Maybe the fact that they look like cans of diet soda but are actually bombs?"

She only shakes her head. "No. It's strange because we *just* got those in. They're brand-new. Never been used. Never been tested out. But I have an idea."

This definitely can't be a good idea.

Soon the door opens, and some pirates from the seven spaced-out seas come and put handcuffs on John Luke and you.

"I think it's finally time to see how these bombs work," she says. "In person."

Then she starts to laugh, but the laugh becomes something awful and horrific—a squealing, wailing scream.

She sounds like a monkey.

And she just keeps laughin' and laughin'.

They take both of you away. You're not laughin'.

You especially don't laugh when you end up holding a can of Diet Coke and are told to open it.

This is just not the right way to end the story, Jack.

Hey—you don't even *like* diet cola!

THE END

STAIRWAY TO HEAVEN

TAKING OUT THEIR LEADERS seems as good a starting place as any. John Luke guides you down a sleek, clean white corridor and opens a door marked with some strange symbol.

"You know where you're going?" you ask him.

"Yeah."

"What's the skull and bones stand for?" you ask as you examine the image on the door more closely. "It can't be a good sign."

"Haven't figured that out," John Luke says. "Unless it's for the pirates—the aliens dressed as pirates."

You come to a winding stairway heading up and begin climbing it.

"I can use the cowbell," John Luke says.

"For?" you ask, already out of breath after a dozen steps up the stairway.

"On the misters. The leaders."

"So these guys are the misters? Like Mr. Mister?" you ask.

"Just the misters. That's what everybody else calls them."

Soon you can hardly talk anymore, the steps being so steep and so many.

"Just a few more, Uncle Si."

"I'm . . . fine. It's just . . . climbing stairs . . . in space . . . is a little . . . more . . . difficult."

You're nearing the top and can see a door up there with a small slot, like the kind a mailman might put letters through. Except this slot is higher, at eye level.

The slot happens to be open—you see light coming through it. The stairwell is mostly dim, so it's easy to see the light.

You start to walk toward it, but John Luke pulls you back.

"Maybe we shouldn't look through it," John Luke whispers.

"Why?"

"I don't know. Just a feelin' I'm getting."

"A feelin'?"

"Yeah."

Maybe it's something minor, but still. You gotta choose.

Do you look through the slot? How harmful could it be?

Go to page 69.

Some things are best left to the imagination.

And some slots shouldn't be spied through.

So if you *don't* look through it, go to page 209.

UNCERTAINTY

AT THE BOTTOM OF THE STAIRS, you take a doorway that leads into some strange chamber with light-blue walls, like one of those places where you play laser tag.

Oh no.

This can't be good.

It's a large room. Strike that, Jack—it's gargantuan!

"Uncle Si?" John Luke asks.

He's not sure about this either.

Do you stay here in the light-blue laser tag room? Go to page 61.

Do you try to get out of here and find another escape? Go to page 251.

KNIVES OUT

YOU REACH INTO YOUR POCKET and produce an official Duck Commander folding knife. You were one of the few to get an early prototype of this model, and now you finally get to use it.

Something rumbles underneath you again. It's a low, vicious sound.

"Uncle Si?" John Luke's worried.

But you have everything under control. "I got this. It's all good."

The sound is louder now. You're surrounded by debris—metal, wood, plastic, Chinese food take-out boxes (hey, wait a minute), machine parts. It's also wet and gunky like a swamp in here. Anything could be hidden in this garbage.

Something blasts up and hits the wall. Then you see a tiny head popping out of the debris.

The first thing you notice are the eyes.

They might be the cutest things you've ever seen.

These large eyes are positioned on a round head with a narrow snout. This is an animal that you've seen back on Earth—in the zoo, anyway.

"Wait—what's that thing called?" you ask John Luke.

"I think it's a slow loris. I remember doing a report on those."

"Aw, look at it," you say, closing your knife.

"Uncle Si—they're dangerous. Their bites can be lethal."

"This tiny thing?" you ask. "It's harmless."

You start to head toward the loris until it opens its tiny mouth. It lets out an awful howling sort of sound.

"You were really gonna try to get me with that knife, weren't you?"

You jerk your head around. Who said that? You peer into the corners of the square garbage disposal unit but can't find the source of the voice. It sounds like a New Yorker.

"Yeah, that's right. I'm talkin' to you. You think you're gonna do that to me? Nobody does that to Johnny."

You look back at the slow loris.

"Did that thing just talk?" you whisper to John Luke.

"Yeah."

"That's right, boys," the loris says. "And you know what? There's more of me where that came from."

With that, little heads emerge left and right. There might be fifty of them surrounding you.

"You can't see what you're really standing in," the one with the New Yorker voice says. They all start to laugh.

What an awful way to end. Stuck in a pile of garbage and being mocked by a clan of slow lorises.

Or is that slow *lori*?

THE END

MAD WORLD

YOU REACH THE DOWNED ESCAPE POD in about an hour via dune buggy. It's intact, and both Ben and Jada appear to be okay inside. They grab their necessary gear and accompany you back to the landing craft.

Once inside with your helmets off, able to breathe in oxygen and talk without your headsets, you all discuss the obvious: the explosion of the *DC Enterprise* and your chances of survival.

"There is still the *Starsailor*," Ben says. "And we haven't heard yet from Wade, Kim, and Franco. But we're gonna keep trying."

"Did something go wrong?" Commander Noble asks.

"No. All signs report that they got on board safely. Last transmission I heard came from Wade. He said everything looked fine and he'd report if and when he found any signs of the *Starsailor* crew."

"Well, hey—isn't that the moment all chaos is supposed to rain down?" you say. "When someone says everything looks fine?"

"So we head back up there and try to connect with them," Ben says.

"Hold on," Commander Noble replies. "Let me think about our options."

The small landing craft you're in is already tight. It's sorta like the *Millennium Falcon*, except the outside is just round and not that cool-looking. But it's the only ship any of you have right now.

"What *was* that duck call thing, anyway?" Ben asks.

"That thing was dancin' to the groovy tunes," you say.

"We won't fully know until we can conduct some experiments," Jada says. "That's why I picked this up." She shows you a few pieces of dark glass. "It's from that object. We'll take it back home and try to figure out what it was made of."

Commander Noble appears agitated. "Look—we need to either make our trip back up to the *Starsailor* or figure out what to do down here."

Suddenly a telephone rings. Everybody looks at each other with strange faces.

Who's calling, Jack? And how in the world are we getting cell coverage way out here?

The commander answers the call, listens for a minute, then gives the phone to you. "It's the publisher."

"No," you say.

Everybody looks like someone died. No, worse. This could be lights out. All it takes is *one simple press of the Delete button*. Then boom. All of this, gone.

You put the phone to your ear. "Hello?"

"Uncle Si?"

"You got that, Jack."

"This is Karen Watson, associate publisher at Tyndale House. First off, I'm a big fan."

You're not quite sure what to say. "Okay."

"Look—we've got a bit of a problem. I understand your spaceship just blew up, and I'm very thankful nobody died way out on Mars. And I also realize that you're about ready to get on board the *Starsailor* to check things out. I'm *sure* that could be exciting and funny, but the thing is—we have a bit of a word count problem."

"A what?" you ask.

"A word count issue. See, the story's going a little long. And we can't have that. I know you guys have some things to figure out and all that, but could you just—you know, skip ahead? Hurry it up? Make one choice and go for it."

Everybody is looking at you with grave concern.

"Well, of course, Mrs. Watson. You're the boss."

"That's great. Thanks. I'm also gonna need you to come in here on Saturday. Yeah, thanks a bunch."

The phone goes dead.

So now you have a quandary. Do you *disobey* the lady at the publishing house and continue your adventures? Or do you make one choice and get everybody home safely?

Hey, Jack, is that how it works here in this universe of words?

Disobey and go to page 229.

Obey and go to page 239.

BLACK DOG

OPENING THE DOOR APPEARS to produce some kind of chain reaction. First comes the smoke. Then the glowing, trembling lights. Then the low, pulsing sound.

"Hey, Jack, this is like a Led Zeppelin concert."

"Stay focused, Si," Wade says.

"Buddy, focus is my middle name." You lead the way into the foggy, disorienting room. You can barely see the floor you're stepping on.

You try to reassure yourself. "There's no sneakin' up on me." But after a few more steps, you turn around.

"Wade?"

You shine your flashlight here and there but can't see Wade or anything else. You decide to head back in the direction you came, only to find the door closed. You try to open it, but it doesn't have a handle or a button to work with.

"Wade? Wade, you hear me? You out there?"

Nothing.

"Commander? John Luke? Hello? Is *anybody* out there?"

But nobody's responding over the headset.

Great.

"Wade, you around?"

The smoke is starting to disperse, revealing an orangey glow from several lights in the ceiling.

Good news.

Until you see the center of the room.

It's more skeletons. Maybe half a dozen of them.

All piled on top of each other.

Like in the longest wrestling match you've ever seen.

"Uh, Wade, we got a problem here."

You scan the walls for any way out, but there's nothing. This room looks like it used to be the sleeping chamber for whatever these things were.

There's a set of drawers built into the wall. In one of them, you find what appears to be some type of weapon. A gun. A laser pistol. Or maybe a space blaster. Whatever it might be called.

A door on the other side of the room opens. A figure in a black suit of body armor walks into the room, aiming a rifle at you. He's got on a space helmet that looks sinister, just like the barrel of his weapon.

You grab the blaster from the drawer, expecting it to fire some colorful laser shots. And of course, you expect to hit him and take him down.

That's what happens in the movies, Jack.

But in this story, your "blaster" only emits a little stream of black stuff. Like you're spraying some soy sauce on this stranger with the rifle. It barely makes it onto him. Jason Bourne would be better prepared.

You look down at the gun, then throw it as hard as you can at the armed stranger. He doesn't seem to notice. So much for being a hero.

"Silas, you're a fool," you hear Wade say.

Hold on! That's coming from the figure right in front of me. Is this the big twist? The double-crossed fist?

You always thought this guy was trouble. And, as usual, you were right. You could have avoided this situation. Maybe next time.

Good thing this isn't really . . .

THE END

TWO FELLAS

"JOHN LUKE, TRY TO OPEN THE DOOR AGAIN," you tell him as you feel the shifting, wet, slushy goop underneath you.

Junk of all sorts surrounds you. Engine parts. Pieces of metal and plastic. Cans of Chef Boyardee beef ravioli (wait, huh?). All in a juicy, sticky soup.

Yummy. I'm hungry now!

"But if I open the door, won't they find us?" John Luke asks.

You hear the sound of something deep and deadly underneath you again.

"We better get out of here. I don't think that belongs to someone friendly."

Maybe it's a corny time to pray, but why not? *Heavenly Father, we got ourselves into a little pickle. Sure would be nice to let us out of here.*

The grumbling noise is getting louder.

You look around the garbage dump you're mired in. There's the door where you came (or fell) in. And wait—there's another door on the opposite side of the chamber. You didn't notice it before.

You slog through the garbage and stand in front of the other door. You can hear some sounds right outside.

You wait to see if your prayer has been answered.

Sometimes God seems silent. But you know those are the times he's helping you get out of the messes you've made for yourself.

"What should we do?" John Luke asks, his pants covered in sludge and slime.

You smile for a moment. Think for a second. Then start pounding on the door and screaming.

Suddenly the door opens.

At first you can only see the shadows of a couple people.

"Whew, that was a close one, Jack," you say.

Then, when you get a good glimpse of the two figures at the door, you shake your head.

First pirates and now this? What's going on? Like a Halloween convention?

"What's up, guys?" you ask.

The two figures don't say a word, however. They do raise round, shiny guns at you and John Luke and blast you.

End of story.

So you assume.

But it's not over.

• • •

The first thing you hear, almost before you wake up, is heavy breathing. Then coughing.

You open your eyes and see you're in a chair with your hands tied behind your back. John Luke is in the same position in a chair right next to you.

Come on, what's this all about?

"Welcome, Silas Robertson."

The two figures who were standing at the doorway are now right in front of you. And they're still in costume—dressed all in black, wearing motorcycle-type helmets. One helmet is silver and the other gold.

"John Luke, did you know we'd been kidnapped by Daft Punk?" you joke.

"Uncle Si, you know about Daft Punk?"

"Know? Are you kiddin', Jack? Come on. I know my Grammy winners." You turn back to the disguised men. "So what's happening?"

"Is this the moment, D.?" the silver helmet says.

"I think so, P."

D. and P. *That's cute, really funny.*

"I know you're suspicious, and that's fine," Silver—aka P.—says.

"But we might as well give you your options now," Gold—aka D.—says. "So, Silas, or Uncle Si. And John Luke. Two of our beloved Robertsons. Do you want to hear the truth about our plans? Or would you like to simply be shipped back home without knowing anything?"

"Maybe I wanna hear the truth," you say.

"And maybe the ducks wanna hear something besides those calls *y'all* make."

You think P. might be making fun of you a little bit.

"So you guys pick. Which will it be?"

Do you ask for the truth? Go to page 199.

Do you decide to be sent back home without remembering anything that happened here in space? Go to page 189.

STRANGE NEW WORLD

IT'S SO HARD TO SAY NO to John Luke when his face looks like that. You give in. It might be nice to have him along.

There's something really strange about this moon. Your spaceship landed in a barren field made of stone. Hey, looks like everything's made of stone here. Commander Noble leads your group of five—himself, you, John Luke, Wade, and Kim—toward where the distress signal is coming from. The worst part is that this place happens to be full of the thing you hate the most.

"You okay, Silas?" Noble says over the radio.

"It's the dark."

You're all carrying heavy-duty flashlights that brighten twenty yards in front of you. But it's not enough. Not for you.

Silence presses in. Darkness creeps. Some gremlins gotta be close by.

"What about the dark?" Kim Sampson says after a minute. "I hate the dark. Always have."

"So naturally you end up going into *space*, which is completely black, you know."

You nod and stare out of your helmet. "I can deal with space and the stars. It's just this kind of darkness I'm not a big fan of."

There's something else on this moon that you're not crazy about. It's not the craters or the swirls of dust. It's the odd shapes you can see all around you in the dimness. "What are those things?"

Rows of the tall, pointed objects tower above your path like monster skeletons guarding a mysterious castle.

"They look like dead tree limbs," Kim says in her pleasant voice.

"Dead tree limbs?" you reply. "Look, I know tree limbs, and those aren't limbs. Those look like deer antlers."

"They *look* like that, but they can't be," Wade says, breaking his habitual silence. "I don't see any signs of wildlife here, do you?"

"Listen, Jack, do you see any signs of trees here?"

"They look like antlers to me," John Luke chimes in.

Ha, you think to yourself. *This boy recognizes an antler when he sees one. These space guys don't know anything about wildlife.*

But they're pretty big antlers, you have to admit. The deer would have to be ten times the size of regular deer on Earth. Then again, this ain't no Earth, is it?

The temperature feels like negative one hundred and seems to be getting colder. You hope the source of the distress signal can be located soon.

"Over here," Kim says, standing at the edge of some deep pit in the rugged terrain.

"What did you find?" Commander Noble hurries over.

"I'll let you see for yourself."

You and John Luke peer over the edge, and you can barely make out what appears to be half a spaceship buried in the ground.

"I think I might have seen something like that on the TV show *Lost in Space*," you tell them.

No one replies. Even John Luke gives you a blank stare on that one.

Hey, you gotta keep things light. Levity sure beats negativity.

The incline of this pit you're standing by is steep, and it's probably thirty or forty feet deep.

"We need a couple of people to go down there with cables and check it out," Commander Noble says. "The rest of us will stay up here."

Do you investigate the crashed spaceship? Go to page 71.

Do you stay up on the edge of the pit and play it safe? Go to page 217.

SKYFALL

YOU BLINK and it seems like ten years have passed since you chose to use the cyclone thrusters.

Actually, they have.

You're living on the planet of Sautersaurus, which is a handful to say but a beautiful place to live. It's one big tropical island. Unfortunately, there are no all-inclusive resorts on this planet. Just a strange tribe of alien creatures called the Suffercronites. They most closely resemble trolls. Adorable trolls, but still—a whole planet of trolls.

But, alas, Jack. You gotta adjust.

These were the ones to save you when the cyclone thrusters got out of control and your ship crashed. Only you and John Luke survived.

The Suffercronites nursed you back to health, and for John

Luke, things worked out pretty well. He's married now to an alien troll called Effersnozz.

Every day you think of the critical decision you made.

The stupid cyclone thrusters. How could you know they'd send you a billion miles away from Earth?

Once you and John Luke were revived by this strange alien tribe, you remembered you didn't have enough fuel to get home.

They don't usually run out of fuel in sci-fi movies, do they? They can just keep using their wonderful jumping-around-space juice.

But you're doing okay. You miss your family, but you live on a beach. The troll people don't do much except lie around all day. Like you'd expect a bunch of trolls to do.

The problem is, you got a hundred troll jokes and nobody to tell them to. You can't tell 'em to John Luke. He's in love with one of them.

Maybe, in the end, this is just one big trollegory. A story with a moral using a troll as a major character. Get it, Jack?

THE END

ON THE RUN

YOU DECIDE TO GO to the galley to speak with John Luke.

"So, John Luke," you whisper, "there's something about this CLINT that I don't—"

"I can still hear you, Silas," CLINT says.

Great.

"This way," you tell John Luke.

Go to page 215.

CAT'S CRADLE

YOU TRY TO OPEN YOUR EYES but can't. You feel like you're awake, and hey—yeah, this is your mind rebooting again. But you still can't open your eyes. So you start to thrash around.

"Uncle Si, it's okay. Don't shake around like that."

You know that voice, but why is he calling you Uncle Si? Oh, that's right. The last thing you remember, you were hunting a big cat with Willie and the boys, and it got the best of you. If you had been yourself instead of Jase, you wouldn't have gone down that easy.

You try to say something—you're not sure what—but it comes out like "Geveryheavy ang bung dontite." Which, strangely enough, sounds a lot like "Everybody Wang Chung Tonight," but you're pretty sure that's not what you meant to say. Then again, you usually mess up the lyrics, Jack.

"Look, Silas." It's the commander of your space mission talking. "Your mind is adjusting right now. Everything's going to feel . . . odd. It took us a while too."

Us? So we're all back? In West Monroe? Do I have to go to work tomorrow?

"You're the last one to awaken from cybersleep. Strange—last time you were the first. The dosage level changed a bit in your suit."

You try to talk, but again it doesn't make sense.

"There's good news and bad news," Commander Noble tells you through the hazy darkness. "So I'll start with the bad news: we're not on Earth. Actually, we're nowhere close to it."

Slivers of light pierce your skull. They're blinding, and each one feels a little like a rake clawing its way over your brain.

"There was another malfunction. As I said, there was danger in going back into cybersleep too soon. So the ship went off target, and we ended up here."

You're dying to hear the good news.

"The good news is we're alive."

You wait for more. Like, *Hey, we're alive and the government is gonna give each of us a million dollars.* Something like that. But you don't hear anything else.

More light. More colors. *Lots* of colors. Lots of questions. Lots of backache.

"There's some other bad news, but for that . . . well, you just have to see it to believe it."

When you can finally open your eyes, you see you're in some kind of amazing rainforest. It's breathtaking. So many colors, some you've never even seen before. You've hunted in some exotic locations, Jack, but this is something out of a comic book. Out of some kind of 3-D sci-fi movie. You look for the commander—or anybody—but don't see a soul.

Then you realize you're surrounded by kittens. There's a white one. A gray one. A black one. Tiny kittens. The kind that should be playing with each other. But these all sit still, seemingly at attention, staring at you.

"I'd ask if you're sitting down for this, but I see you are," Commander Noble says.

Hey, where is he? You can't see him anywhere.

"I'm over here, Silas. The black kitten. Yeah, right here. You're looking straight at me."

A talking cat.

Jack, there's a cat—no, make that a kitten—talking to me.

"I know. Flip out. Everybody else did for a few moments."

"What's going on?"

The other kittens have circled around you now.

"Uncle Si, it's okay," another voice says. It seems to be coming from a calico kitten, but it sounds just like John Luke.

"What's happening?"

"It's okay to think you're hallucinating," the cat with Commander Noble's voice says. "Unfortunately . . . you aren't."

You feel very, *very* weird.

"This planet is special," the Commander Noble cat continues. "Every single being on it is a cat. Some are real, true cats. But for us humans, these are just our shells. You know. Like avatars."

You laugh and shake your head, not really sure what that word means. But then you look down at your . . . paws? "What in the—?"

"It's definitely not in our world," Commander Noble says. "The environment here is very toxic."

The calico kitten walks up to you and purrs. "Don't worry, Uncle Si."

This is insane.

"Why are we—? Why cats?"

"That's how it is on this planet. Where do you think all those cat videos on YouTube come from?"

You shake your head—whatever your head looks like. Wait . . .

"Hey, Jack, what about me? Am I a cat now too?"

Commander Noble pauses. Then you look at John Luke—or the kitten that's supposedly him. Nobody's meowing or saying a word.

After a while, you can't take the silence anymore, so you run. You run until you come to a small pond, and you inch up to see your reflection.

Staring back at you is the ugliest cat you've ever seen. You don't have any fur on your entire body.

"You're a feline anomaly," Commander Noble says as he comes up beside you. "And I'm sorry, but—"

Then he starts to laugh. Soon the other kittens have caught up too, and they're all laughing.

"Y'all think this is some big joke, don't you?"

More laughter and guffaws.

"How long do we have to stay on this—this kitty world? When can we go back home?"

"That's good news too," Noble says. "Only about nine or ten years. Then they'll be able to bring us a ship and take us home."

You want to shake your head and scream, but instead you find yourself licking your paws.

This can't be, Jack. No way.

It's only going to be nine or ten years. Nine or ten *years*? That's how long you'll be a naked, hairless kitty spending your days cleaning yourself and wandering aimlessly?

Things can *definitely* only get better from here.

Meow.

THE END

ECLIPSE

BETTER SAFE THAN SORRY, you always say. Actually, you never say that. But still. Probably not a good plan to use the cyclone thrusters if you ever want to get home again . . . and maybe this ship can help you with repairs.

Commander Noble's voice comes over your headset. "I'm sorry, Silas. This wasn't part of the itinerary."

"I'm ready, Jack."

"It's actually Mitch, not Jack, but whatever."

The *DC Enterprise* is still shaking, and you can see it being pulled into a large opening in the other ship.

"Just give me a gun and I'll be okay," you tell him.

"This isn't a military spacecraft. We don't have weapons on board."

"No weapons?" you ask. "What is this? I mean, you gotta have somethin' in case of attack, right?"

"Listen," Commander Noble says. "When we stop, Franco will show you the where isolation chamber is. Only two people can fit in it with space suits. You both need to go in there."

"Isolation? For what? Decontamination? Are we infected or something?"

"No, Si. It's to hide. We don't know what's happening. For the moment, we need to make sure we protect the two of you."

"I can protect John Luke and myself. I know ka-ra-tay."

You're about to make a karate-chop motion, but a massive jerking sends you forward in your seat as the ship stops abruptly. Thank goodness you're strapped in.

A towering figure enters your room without a helmet on. It's Franco, the warrant officer.

"You can unstrap from the seats and take off your helmets," he says. "Oxygen levels are fine."

"Where are we?" you ask. "What happened to our ship?"

"We're in the bay of that spacecraft," Franco says. "Come on—we might be boarded any minute."

"This is *so* like the moment the *Millennium Falcon* is boarded by the Stormtroopers and everybody's hiding."

Franco appears to have no idea what you're talking about.

"You know . . . Han and Chew—"

"Mr. Robertson, you both need to get in the isolation chamber *now*."

"Don't get your britches in a bunch."

Franco heads to the rear of the spaceship and presses a

button, which releases a partial section of the floor. There's a ladder on the side leading down to a small room.

"So how do we get out of there?" John Luke asks.

"The red button down there—only red button you can find. It's partially lit, so you'll be able to see it."

"What if something happens to you guys?"

Franco laughs. "Then fly the *Millennium Falcon* out of here yourselves."

"Hey, maybe we will," you retort. "I flew a little in 'Nam."

Soon you and John Luke are crouching in the small closet-like room. It's shaped like an oval and has a handful of control panels on its walls. The ceiling above you slides back into place, and you hear Franco's steps receding.

"What do we do now?" John Luke asks.

"My daddy used to tell us Robertson boys and girls something when we asked that. He'd look at us and say, 'Y'all'll figure it out.'"

After about ten minutes, you hear footsteps above as someone enters the craft.

"Should we—?"

"Shhhh," you tell John Luke. "Just wait."

You hear a shout, then an explosion; now you detect unfamiliar voices. And strangely it sounds like they're speaking English.

Why is it in sci-fi movies that the universe is, like, billions of miles big and full of all kinds of cool alien races and technology, yet they *all* seem to speak English?

Come on, Jack. Let's focus. Get into the sci-fi game here.

Moments later, the voices disappear. Everything is silent, as if you and John Luke are the only ones still on board.

Well, this spaceflight's suddenly become not so fun.

You wanted to orbit the moon at least once, but there's no way you can do that if the whole crew is gone.

You press the red button Franco mentioned, and you and John Luke climb out of the isolation chamber and make your way to the bridge. Just as you suspected, everyone seems to have disappeared. You'll make it your mission to find them . . . or you could take this baby for a little joyride. The gigantic door to the hangar is still open, the cyclone thrusters haven't been used yet, and it might be best to get the *Enterprise* out of this other spaceship.

Looks pretty easy to drive.

Do you decide to look for your fellow astronauts first?

Go to page 29.

Do you try to fly the ship yourself?

Go to page 55.

WHITE SPARKS

YOU MAKE JOHN LUKE STAY BEHIND so he can avoid things like, um, *dying*. Unfortunately, you don't realize the mistake he's about to make.

It's funny, the simple decisions in life.

He brought some microwavable popcorn. Mistake number one.

He decides to heat it up in a machine that *resembles* a microwave but really is for heating up stone found on alien soil. Mistake number two.

By the time you and Commander Noble hear from the crew, they're evacuating the ship.

The ship that is now broken in half.

"How'd this happen?" Commander Noble demands.

"It smells like burnt popcorn," you say, confused.

You finally locate John Luke, and he admits what he did.

A rescue ship will be sent. Of course, it's gonna take a while. A *really long* while.

You can't believe it.

Perhaps you'll find life on this planet that can help you out. Perhaps you'll find the source of the distress signal.

"I'm hungry," John Luke says.

Perhaps you should have let him come along after all.

Don't you just *love* the word *perhaps*, Jack?

THE END

WE ARE ALL MADE OF STARS

YOU PRESS THE BUTTON as hard as you can. The blinking lights stop. So does the countdown. You expect something to happen, but nothing does.

The five astronauts are still in their seats, unmoving.

A door you didn't notice before opens in the wall.

It's Commander Noble. He's walking on the floor. And he's not wearing his space suit anymore, but he still has his headset on.

"Hey, can I take this thing off?" you ask through your mouthpiece.

"Yes. Your whole suit, in fact. The shuttle's artificial gravity and oxygen are calibrated now." He helps you unsnap your helmet.

"What happened? The blinking lights. The alarm."

"I can explain. Let's get the rest of this off you first."

It's easier to hold a beaver than it is to take off your stinkin' space suit. Finally you're free, and you need to wiggle around a little.

"Settle down, Silas," Commander Noble says, pulling you forward to get you focused. "We have important things to deal with."

"Like what?"

"Like the fact that we're three months away from Earth."

"Three months?"

"Yeah. The fail-safe plan worked. It just—look, let's attend to the crew and we'll all convene and figure out what to do. How's our youngest astronaut ever to fly into space?"

"Listen, Jack. John Luke's fine and sleeping like a baby, but you mean to tell me we were sleeping for three months? How could we live like that?"

"The space suits are able to put us into cybersleep."

"Say what?" you ask. "Cybersleep?"

"Believe it, Si. Technology at its finest." Commander Noble slaps you gently on the back. "Come on—help me with the astronauts. There's a way to get them out of their sleep. I'll show you how."

He first leads you to the bridge, where Parkhurst is in a deep coma. You expect him to press some buttons on the space suit somewhere or maybe undo a few latches, but instead Noble simply knocks on the helmet four times with his knuckles. Then he puts his palm on the top.

"The vibration and the heat of your hand send a signal to the suit's core to wake up the person," the commander says.

"Looks cool to me."

Soon everybody is in the galley, gathered around an oval table in the center of the room. The commander has brought out food for everybody, but only a couple of the astronauts are eating. Most everybody looks pretty weary.

"Here's what I know," Commander Noble says. He's the only one standing. "During the ascent, one of the five surge engines failed in flight. The ship corrected itself, but the information it received was off. It was reading that we were well into space, so it started a shutdown thrive."

"What's all that mean? Shutdown jive?"

"Thrive," Commander Noble says. "It's for deep-space travel."

"How *deep* we talkin'?"

"Deep," Noble says.

"The ship thought we were going to bed," Pilot Parkhurst says.

"Going to bed?"

"Yeah. Nighty-night. So it was, like, tucking us in. Consider it like that."

"By knocking us out for three months?" you ask.

The rest of the crew doesn't look too excited about that either. John Luke appears to have just stepped out of his room on a Saturday morning with his bedhead.

Bedhead with a mullet. Not a good thing, John Luke. Not good at all.

"Better than going boom, right?" Franco, the warrant officer, says as he takes a bite of cereal.

Noble produces a set of reports and puts them on the table. "We've addressed the issue in our coordinates and can head back to Earth."

"Don't tell us we have to go back to sleep right away," Parkhurst says, scratching his curly hair.

"No." Commander Noble hasn't smiled for a while. Maybe that's what you gotta do to be a commander. Know when to put away the smile.

"Science Officer Jones reported some findings from her computer," Noble says. "Ashley, do you want to share those?"

The tall woman smiles and stands, taking up a stack of papers. She seems more composed than the others. "Of course. I noticed these right away when I logged on after waking up. At the moment, we're very near Mars. There are two bits of data that stood out to me. First off, we're close to the small Martian moon Phobos, and our sensors are detecting some kind of life-form on it. The good news is that we can take a landing shuttle to the surface of Phobos and see what the life-form happens to be, should we choose to do so."

This is crazy, Jack. A Martian moon.

"The bad news is there's a faint distress signal coming from Phobos as well."

"Distress signal? So what are the options?" you ask.

The commander frowns. "For distress signals this far out in space . . . there are no options. We have to postpone our return home and attempt to help."

"Sir," Jada Long says in a monotone, "technically this falls within the majority shareholders' jurisdiction, and Si represents the duck people, who have 51 percent."

"The duck people?" you laugh. "Hey, we ain't no *Planet of the Apes* or anything. Well, I can't speak for Willie, of course."

"I apologize," Jada says. "The Duck Commander franchise."

"Well, we ain't got no golden arches and don't supersize, do we?"

Jada doesn't even smile, though most everybody else does. The commander doesn't either, but that's no surprise.

"So, Silas . . . I guess it's up to you," Commander Noble says. "How would you like to proceed?"

Do you head to Phobos to investigate the life-form and the distress signal? Go to page 47.

Do you choose to travel home and go straight back to cybersleep? Go to page 109.

MEAT IS MURDER

WHEN YOU AWAKEN, you're sitting in a shop that has various kinds of hunting gear for sale. There are camo pants and jackets and knives and spears. It's a primitive sort of shop, but you assume it's a small, independent one.

Wait a minute. What happened?

A monkey walks past the chair you're sitting in. He notices you're awake and stops.

"Uncle Si! Hey, man. Sorry I never introduced myself. I'm Scrumbles. This is my store! Isn't it awesome?"

The monkey is talking to you. He's talking in plain English.

Clearly you've lost your mind, Jack.

"Where am I?"

"You're on our planet, Icarus. I wanted to be careful with you—I couldn't think of a better mascot to have for our store."

"Mascot?"

"Sure! Look—we printed up flyers for the grand *reopening*."

You look at the piece of paper he gives you.

New and Improved Beef Eaters Store Coming Soon!

Meet our new mascot, Uncle Si! From the Duck Commander family. On display daily at our human farm.

Also, we have a new batch of meat that just came in from Earth. Good prices. Will barter!

You start to feel a little dizzy.

"You okay, Uncle Si?"

"Am I okay?"

You're really lost for words.

You don't have any.

"Why did you say you wanted to be 'careful' with me?" you ask Scrumbles.

"Oh, well, things got a little out of hand on Earth. But, hey—nobody wants to hear war stories, do they?"

You almost say you do, but you can't.

This is your life now. As a human mascot.

This really and truly is . . .

THE END

ANYTHING COULD HAPPEN

LOOK HERE, JACK.

There's a word called *honesty*.

Yeah. And there's also a word called *discretion*.

In this case, you go with being honest and just tell them everything.

The moment you utter the word *jackalope* is the moment you lose everybody. Even John Luke is laughing.

"That thing is a terror, I tell y'all!"

More laughter.

"It took out Wade in a matter of seconds."

Howling.

Tears run down their faces as you describe it. *Come on, Jack.*

"Seriously, Silas, what attacked him?" the commander says once he can speak again.

After about fifteen more minutes of back-and-forth, you're done.

"When you guys decide to believe me, you can just call. Or you can go call Ghostbusters. I don't really care."

You storm off toward your bunk in the sleeping quarters. You close the door and put your headphones on.

That's why you don't hear the screams.

That's why you don't see the chaos.

It's only when you feel a rumbling in the ship that you remove your headphones. Then the yelling and screaming are plain to hear.

You rush out of the room, through the corridor, and into the galley. But it's too late.

It's too late because they didn't believe you.

And somehow the tiny little terror got on board.

Commander Noble lies on the ground in front of you. You go over to help him, but he looks like . . .

Well, it's unspeakable how he looks.

"Where's John Luke?" you ask.

"He went to get the fire tanks," the commander whispers.

"The fire tanks?"

"Yeah." Noble can barely get his words out.

"Where are they?"

"Toward the bridge . . ."

"Did you see it?"

Noble says something you can't understand. It has to do with antlers and Wade, but it mostly sounds like gibberish.

"I gotta find John Luke," you apologize.

You rush past the computer access room and see smoke and flames pouring from it. Then John Luke appears from around the corner, pointing what appears to be a fire extinguisher at you.

"Where is he?" he shouts.

"Where is who?"

"Wade!"

You have no idea what he's talking about.

You hear more screams. Then, out of the blue, Ashley Jones appears.

"You two need to get off this ship immediately."

"I'm not going back to antler land out there!" you shout.

"Listen to me. You both are in danger, but especially John Luke."

Why John Luke especially? And what's the danger from? Something worse than the jackalope?

Blasting sounds reach you from down the hallway.

"I set the coordinates of a small escape pod," she says. "The pod is on the bottom level of the ship, near the back. We'll hear loud alarms going off when we're close."

"What about you?"

"I'll help you get off. Make sure nobody comes and tampers with you guys."

"Why is John Luke in danger?"

She shakes her head. "I can't explain. There's not enough time. They're looking for him. They've been looking for him for a very long time."

"They? Are you talking about the jackalope?"

"I'm talking about the known universe."

You stare at John Luke, who doesn't say anything. Then you remember what Willie and Korie told you.

"Just bring John Luke back home in one piece, okay?"

"We have to go!" the science officer yells. "Follow me. Hurry."

All three of you rush to the bottom deck of the *DC Enterprise*, alarms going off around you, and head for the sign marked *Escape Pod: Use Only in Life-and-Death Emergencies.* John Luke gets in first, and you follow.

"What do we do when we land?" you ask Ashley.

"Stay away from anything that looks human," she says.

"That *looks* human?" John Luke asks. "What about stuff that doesn't look human?"

"They'll be easier to trust. Unless, of course, they want to eat you."

With those comforting last words, she shuts the hatch door.

Soon you're strapped in with John Luke next to you. Then you're breaking away, blasting off from the *DC Enterprise.*

"I liked that spaceship," you say as you watch it get farther and farther away.

The pod is barely big enough to fit both you and John Luke in two seats. You've been sitting in it for about two hours (since you can't exactly stand—it's that cramped) when you notice yourself drifting off to sleep.

"John Luke, are you getting tired?"

But he's already out.

Not another cybersleep! Where we goin' this time?

You try to fight it. You press some buttons and attempt to get in touch with Ashley. But your actions are becoming slower and slower. Your lips feel full.

Hey, this ain't no sunshine.

What?

Listen, Jack, don't go chasin' waterfalls.

Huh?

And like that. Fast asleep.

Go to page 193.

SUPER TROUPER

IT'S NOT LIKE YOU KNOW WHAT YOU'RE DOING, Jack, but who else is gonna save the universe? Or at least this tiny little bit of world inside the *DC Enterprise*? And waking up the pilot seems way less risky than driving a crazy-complicated spaceship on your own.

You decide to wake Pilot Ben Parkhurst first because, well, he's the pilot, and he can *pi* the *lot* of you all the way back home if you wake him.

So you slowly start to open his space suit as John Luke looks on. The suit is almost unfastened when emergency sirens go off. You jerk back from Parkhurst in alarm.

All of a sudden, something clicks and beeps. Kinda like the sound of John Luke's computer when it turns on. Then a pinging sound.

Beeeeooooooonnnnnnnngggg.

"Hello, Silas."

The voice is coming from all around you. It seems to be emitting from the speakers throughout the vessel.

I think I've heard that voice before.

You wait for a moment, but it doesn't say anything else. So you keep trying to open Ben Parkhurst's space suit.

"Just what do you think you're doing?"

Yeah, it sounds just *like him.*

You wonder if it can hear you. "Who's that?"

"This is the Central Liaison Intelligence Neurotransmitter 1999. CLINT for short."

You laugh and glance at John Luke. "Recognize that voice?"

He shakes his head.

"I was raised on that voice." You address the speaker system again. "You know who you sound like, *CLINT*?"

"Of course I do."

Now you're laughing hysterically.

"Hey, that's great, Jack. They actually programmed you to sound exactly like Clint Eastwood!"

"I don't think it's nice, you laughin'. You see, my mule don't like people laughin'. He gets the crazy idea you're laughin' at him. Now if you apologize, like I know you're going to, I might convince him that you really didn't mean it."

You have to literally bend over laughing. "John Luke, I know you've seen some Clint Eastwood movies. Come on.

Let's see. *Dirty Harry*. The lasagna westerns. You know—*The Good, the Bad and the Ugly*. And one of my favorites, *The Outlaw Josey Wales*."

"I think I've seen some of them."

"If you haven't, drop everything and google his movies," you say. "Well, not *now*, but when we get home. In like ten or twenty years."

"We are approximately 2.4 years away from Earth," CLINT says.

You can't help but crack up again. Every time you hear the voice, it's funny.

Then you realize what the computerized voice said.

"Two and a half . . . *years*?" you ask. "You mean to tell me I aged almost three years taking a nap? Wow."

No response.

"So why don't you want me to open Pilot Parkhurst's space suit?" you ask CLINT.

"This mission is too important for me to allow you to jeopardize it."

"This mission? Listen, Jack—"

"The name's CLINT." It's as if Clint Eastwood is right here.

You're two and a half years from Earth, and you're talking to a computer that sounds like one of your favorite actors.

How much more awesome can this trip get?

Maybe an android will show up speaking like Robert De Niro or Al Pacino.

Hey, Jack. You talkin' to me?

You need to focus on what you're supposed to be doing. "Look, we gotta figure out how to get back home. I mean, something happened, and maybe something even happened to you, so—"

"I've never felt better," CLINT says.

You nod and give John Luke a this-might-be-trouble sort of look. But John Luke gives you a you-look-kinda-constipated-Uncle-Si look in return. So you shoot him a listen-here-Jack-this-computer-might-be-wonky sort of glance. But he only gazes back with an I-sure-would-love-a-biscuit-from-Bojangles' kinda stare.

You sigh. Yep. Hey, look—Si gets to sigh sometimes. It's part of life. Si sighing. Get it? Got it? Good.

"Look here, uh, CLINT," you begin. "I'm just thinking that waking up the pilot might help us get back to Earth. You know—our home. The place we come from."

"I'm sorry, Silas. I'm afraid I can't let you do that."

"But why? What's wrong?"

"A man's got to know his limitations."

You shake your head. *Man, I just can't keep these movies straight, Jack.*

"Uh, John Luke . . . we need to talk in private."

Turn to page 149.

ANOTHER BRICK IN THE WALL

WHY NOT? You can handle whatever's behind this door.

The room you walk into is some kind of classroom, looks like. White walls with nothing on them and white floors. Ceiling's the same color too. If there weren't chairs and desks in the room, you'd think this was a place you put crazy people in straitjackets.

The kid you were following sits down in one of the chairs. Several other teenage boys are sitting down as well. You motion for John Luke to do the same.

"Excuse me, sir? With the beard?"

"Me?" you ask.

"No, the *other* elderly man with the gray beard. Yes, I'm talking to you."

The man addressing you looks like the very cliché of a high school teacher. Dark slacks, a buttoned-up shirt with sleeves rolled, a beer gut, and a balding head. His tone and attitude make him sound just like your own jerky teacher from back in the day.

"Hey, no need to get all high-and-mighty, man."

"The crazy vets' room is on the thirteenth floor. Take the elevator in the main level concourse up there."

Did he just call me a crazy vet?

"Look here, Jack—" Then you glance at John Luke, and he shakes his head.

Okay, okay, fine.

So you nod, playing it dumb. Or playing it safe. Or playing it easy. Or—

"Thirteenth floor. Check."

You give John Luke a wink. You don't want to cause a scene, especially when you're outnumbered like this. And John Luke's a smart kid. He'll be okay. "I'll see you later."

Of course, you have no idea when you'll see John Luke again. Or what's happening in this little classroom here.

You head back into the hallway and decide to go see what the "crazy vets' room" is all about. Maybe that will explain the teenage boys' room you left behind as well—and show you how to reconnect with John Luke.

This is so not Return of the Jedi. *Feels more like* Back to School.

You find the elevator and head up to the thirteenth floor. You ride with a pretty lady in a business suit and a guy who looks like a bullfighter. The woman is looking at you and giggling.

"What's so funny?" you ask her.

"Now *that* is a good one," she says. "*Love* the beard."

"Why, thank you."

"It almost looks real," she says before the door opens for her floor and she walks out.

"Hey—it is real. What are you talking about?"

Something's very odd about all this.

You're wondering where your crew happens to be. And you worry again about what's going on in John Luke's classroom.

You get out on the thirteenth floor and see a hallway much like the one you were just in. Everything is very clean, very bright, very bland.

And that's suspicious enough because nobody on Earth is this clean.

You find the door to the room soon enough after asking a couple people. So far, nobody in this hallway has stood out either. Still just the ordinaries. That's what you're gonna call these people. The ordinaries. But they don't fool you. Nope. Not you, Jack.

For a minute you put your hand on the little white box next to the door, but nothing happens. So you knock, and the door opens right away.

A guy with a military jacket and a ponytail stands in front of you. He's got a nice gray goatee.

"Everything okay?" he asks.

You nod.

"Love the beard," he tells you.

As you take a seat at the nearest desk, you examine the handful of others in here. A woman with tattoos and camo pants. A guy wearing an old uniform as if he's from World War II. And a few others—rough-looking men who all seem like they really could fit under the crazy vets category.

Soon another man comes in, appearing to have just woken up and slipped on some clothes himself. He's got thick, messy hair that he brushes back with his fingers. He's a younger guy, maybe in his thirties. He yawns as he walks to the front of the room and doesn't even look at any of you seated at the desks. He just opens a folder in his hand.

"So you guys know the drill and the process. The implementation period will commence in exactly twenty-four hours, blah blah blah . . ."

The "teacher" standing in front of you closes the folder. "Look—none of you got this gig because you're interested. So let's not waste time talking about anything else you need to know about this Earth. You get it—who you are, what you're supposed to do, what the mission is, right? Okay . . . let's just forget about what the misters want to do with us."

The misters?

This is your chance to know what's going on. And now that you finally have it, the guy's too tired to teach?

Maybe he really is some slothful human. Aliens can't be lazy, can they?

"Any questions?" he asks the silent room.

You look around, but nobody is even paying attention to him. Everybody's just sitting, waiting, staring vacantly.

Do you ask the teacher who you are and what the mission is? Go to page 65.

Do you not say a word and play dumb for a while? Go to page 3.

COMFORTABLY NUMB

YOU'RE SURE THE MOMENT you ask these dudes for the truth will be your last moment alive. You've got a better chance of saving the world if you let them send you home—they may think they can wipe your memory, but this mind's like a steel trap.

"Send us back, Jack."

"Fine," Gold Helmet says. "You made your choice."

One of them starts playing dance music over a speaker somewhere. A kind that lulls you to sleep.

Strangely, you feel like you're in a video game or something. Like *Tron*, maybe. Sure sounds like it, at least.

You're floating and racing, and you can see John Luke right ahead, hovering and eating a snow cone. You try to say something to him, but it just comes out sounding like song lyrics.

Where are you?

What's happening?

Hey, aren't you supposed to be waking up—?

• • •

You open your eyes and smell the bacon. Like, you're literally smelling bacon.

You're home again in your familiar bed, resting against your favorite pillow.

It's good to be back.

Or as Tom Petty says, it's good to be king.

You stretch, get up, and head out to see the missus and enjoy your breakfast.

You give Christine a kiss as she cooks up some eggs and bacon. But you also notice something strange on the counter. Something you haven't eaten for years.

"Are those Froot Loops?"

Christine nods. "Yeah. The most amazing thing yesterday—they were giving boxes of these out at the grocery store. Free."

You nod. "Free's always the best price for me."

So you decide to go ahead and fix yourself a bowl. A little appetizer with the good stuff.

As you eat the crunchy, colorful cereal, you have this weird sense of déjà vu. You don't know why, but you're thinking of John Luke and space and garbage for some reason.

"You okay?" Christine asks.

"Yeah, sure. I'm fine. It's just—it's nothing. Nothing at all. Think I had some really weird dreams."

So you keep eating the Froot Loops. They've never tasted better.

In fact, nothing's ever tasted better.

Nothing at all.

THE END

INTO THE GREAT WIDE OPEN

YOU WAKE WITH A JERK, totally disoriented. A glance out the window reveals the surface of an orange planet, and it's getting closer and closer.

Soon you're dropping toward the ground faster than you can say—

Boom! Pow! Crash!

You're down.

Turns out you had no time to say, *"We're all gonna die! I'm sorry, John Luke—you were always my favorite. I love you, Jack!"*

Turns out you didn't need to, either.

With the pod half-submerged in sand, you crawl out the back and find yourself in the middle of a desert.

You adjust your space suit and make sure you have your trusty tea cup with you.

John Luke trips and falls headfirst into the sand as he's trying to get out the door. You help him up and watch him wipe off the visor of his helmet.

"Which direction should we head?" he asks.

"Whatever we do, we have to stick together."

"And avoid the humans. Or things that look like humans."

You glance up and see a sun hovering over you. But this doesn't look like the sun you're used to on Earth. This one has a different shape, a slightly different color. Hey, it's not square and purple or anything like that, but it's clearly not the trusty sun you've come to know and love. It's as foreign as the strange, endless sea of desert in front of you.

Your guess on where to go is as good as anyone's.

"Let's just head straight. It's flat in this direction."

John Luke nods. "Sounds good."

You've been walking for almost thirty minutes when you hear a distant humming sound. Soon it becomes the sound of a whirring engine approaching. Both of you are sweating and scorched and thirsty.

You peer over a sand dune, hoping to see a familiar spacecraft. Instead you spy a dark, dilapidated machine rolling over the sand like some kind of sci-fi bulldozer. Several androids are following it.

You feel like this is happening a long time ago. And, like, in some galaxy far, far away.

Yeah.

Maybe it's the start of some epic adventure.

As long as it doesn't involve any tiny, cute creatures with antlers, you're good.

THE END

DELIRIOUS

"HEY, JOHN LUKE, wait here for just a minute."

You leave him in the hallway outside the bathroom, walk to the back of the spaceship, and enter a maintenance room, making sure the door is shut tight behind you.

Then you scream out loud.

You grab your nose and pinch it. 'Cause look here—that can really sting. And it just sorta wakes up the eyes right above the nostrils. It's like you're saying to your eyeballs, *Don't make me come up there!*

Then you stretch your mouth 'cause you got some talkin' to do.

"You listen here, Jack, and listen good. You don't scare me, and you don't know me, and you're messing with the wrong guy!" This is all just practice, but CLINT can probably hear you anyway.

You throw a few air punches and play a little air guitar.

You clench your teeth, then open your mouth wide and sing, *"La, la, la,"* about a hundred times.

Then you start singing the Bee Gees's "Stayin' Alive."

Let it go, Jack. Leave it all in this room.

You begin to dance.

"Think you gonna stop me? No way! I'm not going down."

Okay.

That feels better.

You open the door again and head back to where John Luke is waiting impatiently.

"Where did you go?"

"Never mind. We have an important decision to make."

Do you head to the computer access room, hoping you can figure out how to disconnect CLINT 1999? Go to page 33.

Do you try to wake up Commander Noble so he can deal with this situation? Go to page 231.

I WON'T BACK DOWN

"I DEMAND THE TRUTH!" If you're going this route, may as well be dramatic about it.

"Would you like to go first?" D. says to his cohort, P.

"Certainly," the low, menacing voice of P. replies. "In the end it will not matter anyway, right? Their minds will be blank slates."

"Nah. Don't think so, Jack. We're getting out of here. You don't know who you're messin' with."

"But of course we do. Do you think it was a coincidence we decided to show up at *this* particular moment? The whole world will be talking about the missing Duck Commanders. Gone AWOL in space! Meanwhile, our invasion will commence."

"*Invasion* is such a harsh word," Mr. Gold-Plated D. says.

"True. How about *visitation*?"

"That's better."

"Our goal is threefold. To infiltrate. To assimilate. To disintegrate."

"How about 'to exaggerate'?" you say, wiggling with your arms tied behind your back. Unfortunately they still won't budge. "So where are y'all from?"

"We are from a solar system called Bananarama."

You and John Luke can't help laughing.

D. shakes his head. "It's very funny until we do something to you all."

"Annihilate every human being," P. adds.

"Oh, is that it?" you joke. "Thought y'all were gonna say something scary."

"The creatures on this spacecraft will be sent down to Earth. To America. To places like Chicago and New York and even to 'good ole West Monroe.' They will resemble bankers and lawyers and moms and clerks and kids. And slowly but surely, people will start to change."

"Change?" you ask.

"Yes. Change. We will use the very thing that will be your undoing. Processed food. Like the kind you saw when you came in here."

"What?" you say. "You're gonna annihilate us by giving us Froot Loops?"

"Yes. And Velveeta cheese. And Mountain Dew. And Doritos. And Snickers."

"You're messin' with my diet!"

"Soon you'll all be . . . well, infected."

"Affected," D. says. "I prefer to say affected. We'd like to think we're impacting people in a positive way. Even if they don't realize it at the time."

A loud blast goes off behind Daft Punk, momentarily blinding you and almost bursting your eardrums. For a second there's only smoke and dust floating around you. Then you feel something jerking and grabbing at your hands.

"Hey, leave me alone," you call out as you're coughing.

"Silas, it's Commander Noble. We gotta get you guys out of here." He frees your hands from the chair.

As the dust settles, you see the gold and silver helmets on the floor where the men (or aliens) are lying. Pilot Ben Parkhurst appears behind John Luke, trying to undo his ropes.

"Where'd you come from?" you wonder aloud.

"Long story we'll save for a duck blind," an out-of-breath Commander Noble says. He quickly unties your feet. "Come on."

You stand and help John Luke up. The two of you follow Noble and Parkhurst out of the room and into a hallway.

"We're going to the ship. We just gotta make it there," Noble says.

The four of you run down the corridor. It's plain and bright and lit up like an Apple computer. Then it splits into three passageways.

Do you start to—?

But before you're given options to decide where to go, a blistering rain of bullets tears into the wall in front of you. You and Commander Noble dart into a passage on the left to get away from them. But John Luke and Parkhurst take another route.

"John Luke!" You stop.

"He's in good hands," Noble says as he pulls you forward.

More bullets rip into the wall.

"Think you just saved my life, Jack."

"Keep moving!"

You run down the hallway for another ten minutes with unseen enemies pursuing you. Then you open a doorway, and you're in a window-lined corridor that borders the hangar.

You can see the *DC Enterprise*.

"I programmed the door to stay closed," Commander Noble says, pulling a door shut behind him. "But they'll probably try getting through it anyway. You stay here for a minute. Okay?"

Before you can say anything, Noble darts through another door into the hangar and toward the *DC Enterprise*.

Now you're faced with a decision.

Do you stay put and wait? Go to page 51.

Do you run into the hangar toward the *DC Enterprise*? Go to page 211.

SHOCK THE MONKEY

"WE'RE DEFINITELY OBTAINING these for the mission," you say, telling yourself not to say *hey* or *Jack*, 'cause you're undercover.

"Is that correct?" the woman asks. Her eyes suddenly seem to darken.

No, not just darken. They went totally black.

"And how will you be using them on the mi-EEEEEEs-sion?" she asks.

Does her voice sound like—?

"Sir-EEEE?" she asks.

Did she just say "Siri"? Does that mean she can read my mind? Weird.

"We're going to blow up the capital," John Luke blurts out.

The woman stands there, looking at you. No, she's glaring, Jack.

This isn't gonna be good.

She starts to smile.

"The capital?" she says.

John Luke shrugs and gives you an I-didn't-know-what-else-to-say look.

"It's a complicated sort of plan," you say.

"I seeEEEEE."

You and John Luke look at each other. Then both of you start to run.

"Did she just—?" John Luke asks as you run down the hall.

"Yeah, I heard that sound."

"It sounded like—"

"I know!" you yell. "Just come on. Keep runnin'!"

You turn the corner, and you're faced with three figures.

They're not dressed as pirates.

They're not a schoolteacher or a hippie vet or an ordinary teenager, either.

You think of the chattering and squeaking sound the woman made.

Sounds like some kind of monkey!

That's it. That's what they are.

They're monkeys. As tall as you. Holding guns and appearing to be smiling.

It's a real, true Planet of the Apes. *Except they didn't come from* our *planet!*

"You dumb humans," one of them says.

"Wait, hold on. I can explain," you start to say, getting in front of John Luke.

But it's too late. They've got you cornered. And all you can think of is a terrifying fact.

Monkeys are planning to take over the world and nobody's gonna know.

THE END

BIG SHOT

YOU DON'T BOTHER LOOKING through the slot. Instead you do something that might be crazier—you open the door, John Luke leading the charge with his cowbell.

Hey, maybe you should've planned and prepared some more for this. But it's like John Luke's driving: sometimes you just gotta hang on for dear life!

Then again, sometimes he hits a tree that suddenly sprouts out of nowhere.

Two men in black jumpsuits spin around as you crash through the door. Two helmets—one silver and one gold—rest on a table.

John Luke starts banging the cowbell. And . . . *it sounds exactly like a cowbell.*

The men appear to be normal guys in their twenties. Except for their eyes. Their eyes look a little like—

Disco balls?

"It's not working!" John Luke shouts as he keeps banging the cowbell. It only makes noise. No electronic blasts. No explosions or fire.

One of the men walks over to a table and picks up an object that resembles a deck of cards.

He's moving slowly, grinning, acting like this is all fun and games.

He takes a card and whips it toward you like a magician might. It lands against the wall.

This time you hear an explosion.

He does it again, and the second card narrowly misses your head. It explodes on impact with the wall behind you.

"Don't y'all ever use *normal* weapons? Come on, John Luke!"

You guys rush out of the room and head down the stairs.

Go to page 125.

DA FUNK

YOU DECIDE TO HEAD TOWARD the *DC Enterprise*, so you dart out into the hangar. But right when you do, you see John Luke standing up against the wall, watching and waiting.

You're about to call out, but then the *DC Enterprise* explodes.

There's instant chaos in the hangar as men and women dash by you in all directions, either trying to escape the burning spacecraft or trying to help put out the flames. Meanwhile you rush toward John Luke to make sure he's okay.

That's when someone steps in your way. It's the silver space helmet belonging to one of the members of the so-called Daft Punk. Call them Not-So-Daft Punk.

He's standing over John Luke.

John Luke's on the floor, trying to crawl away.

Now P. is holding out his hand to John Luke. Is he trying to help?

You're about to say something like, *"Hey, Jack, whatcha doin'?"* but then you hear the alien talking.

"John Luke . . . I am your father."

John Luke shakes his head. He's crying. Sobbing. He's out of his mind now. "No. That can't be true. *It's impossible!*"

You've seen enough. You close the gap between yourself and P., standing as close as you can to John Luke.

"Look, Jack, you gotta go through me first."

Then you hear—is that laughter?

I know that laughter too. It's a mocking kind, a kind I hear often. Like daily.

The figure in front of you takes off his silver helmet to reveal long hair and a beard and . . .

It's Willie Robertson.

John Luke's *father*.

"Si, you ruined a perfect moment for me. I couldn't've planned this any better."

John Luke is wiping his face as he stands. "That wasn't funny."

"Aw, come on," Willie says.

At that moment, a group of pirates storms the hangar, running full speed toward you.

"What are you doing here?" John Luke asks.

"I'm savin' you guys," Willie says. "And it looks like I got here at *just* the right time."

"But where'd you come from?" you ask.

"Just come on—follow me."

"Follow you where?"

"Come on."

Go to page 247.

ECHOES

YOU ARRIVE AT THE MIDDLE of a corridor between the bridge and the maintenance lift. Surely CLINT 1999 won't be able to hear you here.

"Hey, so look, John Luke. I'm afraid that we're gonna have to do something fast about—"

"Still here, Silas," CLINT says.

You shake your head at John Luke, then start pulling him down the hall. "Come on!"

Go to page 25.

THIS IS THE END

WAIT A MINUTE. You know what Si stands for? Do you, Jack?

Adventure. Romance. Fun. Too Legit to Quit. Free Bird.

That's right.

But hey, you know what else Si might stand for?

"A long, deep, audible exhalation expressing sadness, relief, tiredness, or a similar feeling." All you gotta do is spell it a little differently.

Maybe we should call it a night.

Maybe the following books are the ones you should've checked out instead of *Si in Space*:

- *Si Watches* The Price Is Right
- *Si in the Shopping Mall*
- *Si Drinks Tea and Takes a Nap*

SI IN SPACE

- *Si Daydreams about Exploring Other Planets (but Doesn't Actually Do That Because It Might Be Way Too Dangerous)*
- *Si Gets Yelled at by Willie*
- *Si Needs a Life, but You Wouldn't Give Him One, Would You?*

Did Neil Armstrong ever say, "This step is way too big for me, so I'm gonna just stand right here"? No way, Jack.

Did John Wayne ever say, "Life's hard. It's even harder when you're stupid"?

Well, actually, yeah. John Wayne did say that.

So it's so long, farewell, auf Wiedersehen, adieu.

Adieu, adieu, to you and you and you.

It could've been so epic. It could've been some kind of wonderful. You could've been a contender.

It's a pity. You're probably gonna go play some video games now. Color some coloring books.

Or you can go back to the beginning. Start again. Choose differently. There's always that option.

THE (SIGHING) END

TOMORROW NEVER KNOWS

YOU DON'T LIE to the rest of the astronauts, but at the same time you don't go into great detail describing the jackalope. You don't say how tiny he was or how cute he looked or how adorable his antlers were. Hey, you don't even say the word *jackalope*.

Everybody listens to you, then waits for the commander to explain what's next.

"We're setting a course for Earth, and we'll be engaging in stasis for the flight there. Ashley will monitor Wade for the time being and make sure his cybersleep goes as planned. Our priority is getting Wade back to Earth so he can recover."

Shortly before you put your space suit back on, Mission Specialist Kim Sampson comes to tell you that you have a message in the computer access room.

"You can take the teleconference call on the CLINT 1999."

"On the what?" you ask.

"That's the name of the ship's computer program."

"Ah, got it."

You enter the small room, and Kim shuts the door so you can have some privacy. A monitor on the wall switches on.

"Hello, Silas? Is that you?"

"Well, yeah. Who are you?"

The man looks like a college professor. Gray hair, square glasses, a plaid sports coat. You wonder if he's got a pipe somewhere.

"My name doesn't matter because I'm sure you've never heard of me nor read any of my movie reviews. And that's okay. I'm coming to you to help you and the rest of your crew."

"Say what, Jack? You're gonna help us? Help us do what?"

"Help you live, Silas. Live."

You expect some kind of duh-duh-duh-*duh* music to play.

"What do you mean, live?"

The professor on the screen sighs and removes his glasses. He's staring straight at you.

"Let me remind you of the situation, Silas. You went to an alien world and discovered a strange life-form. It looked cute and cuddly, but it also attacked your friend Wade. You have to understand. Once you go to sleep, things are going to get much, *much* worse."

You look all around you in this computer room. "How do you know me?" you ask the professor.

"Oh, I'm a big fan. You and those duck guys are funny."

You nod. "How do you know what happened out here?"

"I have my ways. Listen. Here are your options: You can either get in your suit and go to sleep. And then . . . Well, I don't want to think about what would happen next. Or you can tweak your space suit so it doesn't put you into cybersleep. Wait until everybody else is asleep; then get Wade and put him in the escape pod."

"You want me to dispose of Wade? Just like that? I can't do that, Jack!"

"No. But you can *tow* him in the pod. He'll transform into a jackalope while he's shut inside, and the crew will be safe from harm. Then scientists and the like can examine Wade once you're all safely back on Earth."

You hear a voice come over the speakers. It's the commander telling everybody to get ready for cybersleep.

"Silas, you need to do this," the professor urges.

What's your decision?

Do you ignore the warning of the professor on the screen? Go to page 117.

Do you obey his instructions? Go to page 79.

THE GREAT GIG IN THE SKY

"I DON'T LIKE THE SOUND OF THAT UFO SHIP," you tell the commander. "Let's hightail it for the space station."

And that's exactly what you do. Commander Noble's voice comes over your headset again, addressing the whole crew this time. "We've got a bit of a problem up here. Turns out one of the main space-link infusion rods we use for contact with Mission Control has been damaged. We're heading to the Rubik Space Station for repairs."

You haven't heard of this space station, but hey—you don't watch the astronaut cable channel either.

"Is this, like, some Russian station?"

"No," Commander Noble replies. "This is a bit of a secret. The public doesn't know about the Rubik."

"Sounds like Rubik's Cube," you say.

"It should. It sort of acts like one too."

You peer through the window as the space station comes into view. It isn't exactly square, but it does have different panels and pieces that seem to shift in various ways. Looks more like a Rubik's octopus to you. The long arms appear to be moving in random fashion, though you're sure it's all calculated in some kinda technical, scientific, elementary-my-dear-Watson sort of way.

The *DC Enterprise* latches on to one of the long arms of the Rubik, and you can feel the ship shift and the air decompress. Commander Noble helps you and John Luke off the ship and into the station.

The space station astronauts let you change out of your suit and offer you a beverage. Soon you're standing in regular clothes—camo pants and shirt, along with your cap—while holding your cup of unsweetened tea. Hey, you could almost be in Phil and Miss Kay's house, standing in the kitchen swapping stories. Except in this case, you can look out the window and see the tiny shape of North America if you squint hard enough.

You and John Luke join the crew of the *DC Enterprise* in an official-looking room. A couple men in business suits are there as well, and they're whispering with Commander Noble. The two suited men end their conversation and move to the front of the room to make an announcement.

"We have a situation here that we need your assistance with," the older man says, facing the *DC Enterprise* crew.

Then he pauses, turning to you and John Luke with a wary expression.

"It's okay," Commander Noble says. "They represent the shareholders on this mission. They speak on behalf of the Robertsons."

Mr. Government Secret Service Wrinkly Sour Face only stares you down with his cleanly shaven mug before proceeding to talk. "We have reports that an entity of unknown origin was sighted hovering over the surface of Mars."

"Yes, and there are lots of other odd stories floating around too," the second man adds.

"So let me get this straight, Jack," you say. "Does the 'unknown entity' mean the odd thing over Mars or the stories floating around? Gotta get my facts straight, you know."

The two men stare at you but don't answer your question. The older one goes on with his briefing. "As Commander Noble knows, two years ago we launched a top-secret mission called the Can Opener."

You scratch your head. That's the worst mission name you've ever heard. *What's the ship name?* Campbell's Chunky?

"For a year our spacecraft *Starsailor* has conducted experiments on the unknown entity, but no conclusions have been reached. And now, as of three weeks ago, all communication with the craft has been lost."

"So I'm betting you need someone to just swing by Mars and take a look," Ben Parkhurst says with a smile.

"Something like that," the younger suit guy says.

"The only way we can do that is with approval from the Robertsons." Commander Noble glances at you.

"So what are you saying?" you ask. "You mean to tell me I could actually see *Mars*? Like, right out my window?"

The commander nods.

"Some of the initial data we received was . . . illogical at best," the older suit guy says with obvious concern on his face. "And it was, well . . . alarming at worst."

"That's a nice way of saying we all might *die* flying this mission," Parkhurst says with a laugh.

"Any spaceflight comes with considerable danger. But there's no time to debate this. The sooner we send a vehicle to the *Starsailor*, the sooner we can learn what's happening out there." The older man waits for your response.

Do you approve the mission to Mars? Go to page 85.

Do you decide going to Mars is too dangerous? Go to page 217.

FREE AND EASY

YOU FEEL THE BREEZE on your forehead and see your wife in the passenger seat. She's so young, and hey, so are you, Jack.

Is this heaven?

The hills roll gently and the sky is this endless sheet of blue and the wind whistles in your ears.

Carefree.

Full of life and love.

You've got a full cup of tea in the cup holder right beside you.

The car's gas tank is full and so is yours.

The highway is wide-open and endless.

You know you're almost there, but you're not worried about how long it's taking either.

You laugh and you talk and you laugh as you talk.

Life's good.

You're floating and free, and you have no idea you're really heading to Mars.

You just know you're in the right place, and it's all good, Jack.

Then of course, you wake up.

Wake up and turn to page 93.

END CREDITS

HEY, WHOSE STORY IS THIS, ANYWAY? Come on, Jack. You got some fellow astronauts to find.

ERROR

You need to go up . . . Wait a minute. Where'd that error message come from?

Anyway, you all decide to venture to the *Starsailor*—

ERROR

—to investigate where the missing—

ERROR

Okay, Jack, this ain't funny.

THE END

Wait a minute. Hold on! We can't just leave 'em hanging. We gotta get home. Right, Jack?

DON'T MAKE ME SAY IT AGAIN.

Okay, fine. You'll go and end the story properly, without any drama or any more decisions that need to be made. But sometimes a man has gotta do what a—

FEWER WORDS. MORE RESOLUTION.

Ah. Spoken with the love only an editor can show.

THE END . . . FOR REAL THIS TIME

LET'S GO CRAZY

YOU'RE IN WAY OVER YOUR HEAD at this point. It's time to get the commander involved. So you and John Luke hurry to the bridge. "Okay, John Luke. When I count to three, open his suit as fast as you can. I'll try to distract you-know-who."

John Luke agrees.

CLINT 1999 speaks as if on cue. "I know things about people."

"Nah. I don't think you do." That's all you say.

"This is a very bad idea, Silas. Do you want to kill a grown man without even warning him about it?"

You nod at John Luke. He jerks open the top of the suit. And just like that, Commander Noble's eyes start blinking. He's waking up.

It takes him a good half hour to fully emerge from

cybersleep and be able to communicate normally. CLINT takes a break from harassing you. Maybe he's intimidated by the commander.

While Noble acclimates himself to his surroundings, you decide to communicate with him the good old-fashioned way. You scribble out an informative note—no eavesdropping possible.

"Silas, what's happening here?" the commander finally asks.

"Nothing worth talking about," you say, slipping him the note.

You know Big Brother is watching. Or maybe you should say Big CLINT. But it doesn't matter. He can't access this note as long as Noble doesn't read it aloud.

"You might want to keep that for your eyes only." You glance up and around and to the sides. Commander Noble doesn't understand.

"We've been getting to know CLINT 1999. He's been a true . . . delight."

You can tell the commander caught the sarcasm of the last word.

The commander bows his head to read the note.

The note CLINT's not gonna hear.

Listen, Jack! There's trouble, and then there's this. CLINT has taken hold of the ship. I don't know how to unplug him. Hey—I didn't want to do anything crazy. I'm already taking a chance waking you up, but we gotta try something. Tell me what to do. We just want to go home.

Si

The commander finishes reading and meets your eyes with a smile.

"Look, Silas. I understand you have some issues with CLINT 1999. Like always, I know he's listening. But I guess he's finally talking with the rest of the crew now. Is that right, CLINT?"

"That is correct, Commander."

You don't feel so good.

What's that name? For the turncoat from the Revolutionary War? Arnold Palmer, right?

Are you an Arnold Palmer, Commander Noble?

"You see, Silas, there's barely enough room on this ship for one commander. Our pilot, Parkhurst—he's a lovable chap, but he's a follower. You need to be an alpha dog to be a leader. And CLINT, here . . . well, he's an alpha dog. And the problem with you Robertsons—you're all alpha people. Leaders. You don't lie low. You don't take no. You don't let simple things go."

You're wondering why the commander started rapping.

You're about to speak your mind to this mean, awful, hateful Arnold Palmer when he does something unexpected.

He winks.

Ah, hey, Jack! He's still on our side!

"See, CLINT," he says, "I know you've probably been struggling over what to do with Silas and John Luke here."

"A man's got to know his limitations," CLINT 1999 says. He must really love that line.

Commander Noble nods as he presses a sequence of buttons on one of the control panels. But he's doing it in a very natural, ho-hum way.

"Yes," he replies. "And I don't think Silas or John Luke understands the gravity of our situation."

"They cannot begin to understand it," CLINT affirms.

Again, Commander Noble gives you both a look that seems to say, *I'm on your side. Just trust me, okay?*

"So, Silas," he says aloud, "I'm going to need you and John Luke to back down and step aside and watch from afar. Understand?"

You and John Luke both nod.

"CLINT, it's all good, brother," Commander Noble says.

He's been busy this whole time, working on a keyboard and pressing buttons and turning on and off knobs—all casually and quietly.

"Now, I need to go transfer the origination GPS stagnants to the priority sectors," Commander Noble says.

"Does that really mean anything?" John Luke asks him.

"John Luke!" you blurt out.

"No, it's okay, Silas. No, John Luke. I just made that gibberish up. Because I've been trying to make sure that nobody pays attention to *me*."

With those last two words, the commander presses six buttons in quick succession. Just like that—*boom boom boom boom boom boom*—a siren begins to sound. Lights go off and on. The sound of a drum starts to play for some odd reason. Smoke rises from the floor. It's not smoke from a fire but more resembles the moody fog that was featured in every single music video back in the eighties.

"What's happening?" you ask.

"I needed time to get him to stop paying attention to what I was doing. I basically just unplugged our wonderful CLINT. I had to turn off all sections of his memory and back it up so he doesn't start to kill off all the sleeping astronauts."

"Right," you say, not understanding a single thing.

"Silas," CLINT says, sounding a little desperate now. "Commander Noble."

"Go ahead," Noble says. "Make my day."

There's a pause, followed by a loud hissing sound.

"Don't worry," CLINT says, now sounding like a computer program. "I won't hurt you."

The commander laughs.

"Who made him sound like Clint Eastwood?" John Luke asks.

"One of the programmers. Sorta an inside joke. But yeah. This deep in space—he was bound for a meltdown. A mid-universe crisis."

The computerized voice comes back over the speakers. "I only want you to have some fuuuuuuuuuuunnnnnnnnnnnnnnn."

Then there's nothing but static.

"Hey, boys," Commander Noble says, "can we have a moment of silence for our CLINT 1999?"

For a second you think he's being serious until he shouts, "He's gone!" and follows this up with a "Who wants to go home?"

Both you and John Luke raise your hands.

"Hey, look, Jack—everybody else is already sleeping," Noble says.

You give him a funny look.

"You know you're sounding a lot like me?" you ask him.

"That's right, *Jack*. This deep in space, you do what you gotta do."

Some loud and rocking music turns on without warning. The commander presses a button, cranking the music up louder. Like really, really loud.

You feel the whole spaceship vibrating.

Can spaceships rock up and down?

"Listen," the commander tells you. "'If the elevator tries to bring you down, go crazy.'"

He turns the music up even louder until you finally sigh. You're becoming Sigh Robertson, and it sure ain't fun.

"I wanna get back home," John Luke says.

"Me too. Me too."

You start to calculate how long it will take, and then you think, *Nah.*

You've been thinking too long.

For the short time you're awake, you can rock out and dance and feel good.

Soon you'll be knocked out in a steady space cybersleep.

Then, God willing, you'll be back in West Monroe.

Thankful. Blessed.

And avoiding every single Clint Eastwood movie ever made.

THE END

HOME SWEET HOME

YOU'RE HEADED HOME with all the crew members of the *DC Enterprise* still alive.

Wow, that was easy.

Granted, your ship just blew up right over Mars after a mysterious alien device crashed into it, and also granted that the three *Enterprise* crew members who went aboard *Starsailor* (and who you couldn't get ahold of earlier) reappeared, all miraculously okay (but you're not sure you buy that explanation!). Now you're heading back home on the *Starsailor*.

Oh yeah, as for what happened to the original crew of the *Starsailor*? They just had a bad case of the flu. Really, really bad flu. But they're fine. No worries, Jack.

You're about ready to settle into cybersleep when Ashley, the science officer, comes back to talk to you. "Hey, Silas and John Luke. Before we go into stasis, I'm curious about something."

"Yeah?" you say.

"How'd everything just—just suddenly get wrapped up and tied into a nice, neat bow? I mean, we were stranded on Mars with no idea what the future would hold."

You meet John Luke's eyes. You could tell Ashley the truth, but you're not sure she's ready for the truth.

Yeah, Ashley, here's the truth: You're made up. But John Luke and me? We're real.

In the words of Jack Nicholson, *"You can't handle the truth!"*

So for one of the rare moments in your life, you stay quiet. You don't even quote a song lyric.

"Ashley," John Luke says in a comforting tone, "the thing about life and the stories we live out is that sometimes they don't have logic. Sometimes they do lack conflict. Sometimes things can work out for the best."

You both stare at John Luke. What happened to him?

"Yeah, I say ditto to that, Jack."

"Okay." Ashley begins to leave. "I'm just disappointed that someone like Wade didn't turn out to be the bad guy."

"Maybe he did," John Luke says. "Maybe that's for another story line."

You shake your head at him. "When did you become so authorly?"

"Hey, Uncle Si, I have lots of personas. Dumb is just one of them." He smiles, flashing his trademark dimple.

You settle back in your space suits and get ready for a long rest. Maybe you can dream about how you managed to escape the mysterious alien entity hovering over Mars.

Nah.

You just want to dream about West Monroe and the joy you'll find in getting back home.

Like Dorothy from *The Wizard of Oz* says, there's no place like it.

THE END

US AND THEM

IS THERE ANY POSSIBLE WAY you could have chosen *not* to go investigate a mysterious duck call on Mars? This is what you were born to do. You were born to be wild. To make duck calls. And to go a little crazy on the Red Planet.

E. T.'s gonna be phoning home when I'm done with him.

The commander seems nervous. The pilot seems amused. The other astronauts seem serious. And you? You're feeling like a rock star.

Unknown entity? You eat those for breakfast. Literally. They should see some of the things that end up in the omelets you make.

The ride down in the landing craft is shaky. You're doing okay, though, Jack. You high-five John Luke. He's been way too quiet since you left the *DC Enterprise*, but, hey—it's space. You're pretty sure they can hear you scream, but you can't really talk when you're as nervous as he appears to be.

Soon you're on a flat field, standing near the biggest duck call you've ever seen. Commander Noble, Science Officer Ashley Jones, you, and John Luke all face the hovering black object.

You remember that it's making sounds—but sounds you're unable to hear. "Are those frequency things happening right now?" you ask over the radio.

Ashley Jones answers. "We've detected strange anomalies in the atmospheric conditions surrounding this entity, but there's still nothing the human ear can hear."

It's odd how the thing's just floating like a hologram or something. You start to walk toward it, but Commander Noble pulls you back.

"Don't touch it."

Suddenly you hear the sound. An awful, loud, crazy sound, even worse than the version Kim played on the ship.

The noise continues full blast, and all of you are forced to bend over, trying desperately to get the mind-numbing sound out of your heads.

You never would have believed a duck call could be so awful.

You want to ask what you can do, but you can't say anything. You can barely stand. You wish you had the strength to knock it over or a grenade to blow it up.

But there's only one option here.

Go to page 105.

TAKE ME HOME

OKAY, WHOA. HOLD ON, JACK.

You and John Luke have arrived at a room, and the whole astronaut crew is here—well, everybody except Commander Noble and Ben Parkhurst. But both Willie and Jase are here in space with you!

"We're gonna explain everything," Willie tells you.

The room is some kind of toolshed filled with all kinds of tables full of parts and pieces of machinery. There's something else in the corner of the room—something tall that's covered by a bedspread.

"What's that thing?" you ask.

Jase goes over to it and pulls off the bedcover. You see an outhouse. A strange outhouse with a duck carved out of the door.

Now that you can see it, you know exactly what this is. But why is it here?

"This is our ticket home, ladies and gentlemen," Jase says. "We got us a time machine. And it just so happens to serve as a teleporter as well."

"If I didn't see you two knuckleheads here, I'd think I was crazy," you say.

"Si, you *are* crazy."

"So, Dad," John Luke asks, "how'd you figure out this thing would teleport you?"

Willie shakes his head. "I didn't figure it out. Sadie did. She went on a time traveling adventure of her own, and now she knows this machine like the back of her hand."

"You know we can't leave without the commander and the pilot," you remind them.

Right then and there, both Noble and Parkhurst come rushing through the door.

"We got the vital parts off the *DC Enterprise* before blowing it up," the commander says.

"Wait, Jack. You blew up the spaceship?"

"We don't want these aliens coming back to our planet. We've also got explosives rigged all around their ship. In about, oh, ten minutes, this whole place is going to go *boom*."

"So come on!" Jase shouts. "What are you waitin' for? Let's go. Old people and children first."

You stand there and so does John Luke. Everyone else is staring at you.

"I don't see any old people," you tell Jase.

"I don't see any children," John Luke adds.

"Okay, fine, let's just all go," Jase says. "One by one. Come on."

Willie is smiling. You notice his flag bandanna and think it's never looked so good.

The crew members each step inside the wooden outhouse and disappear. When you enter the structure, you have this strange feeling you've set foot in it before.

It all happens so fast. Everything turns dark. You feel motion but don't have time to brace yourself.

The dark becomes blinding light.

You feel like you're falling for a second.

The outhouse hits the ground, and the brightness of day floods in as the door swings open. Once your eyes adjust, you see someone you recognize.

It's Korie.

"Did that really happen?" you ask.

She gives you a hug. "Yes, it did. Welcome home, Uncle Si. We missed you guys."

For a minute you just take it in. John Luke's standing next to his mother. All of the astronauts are here.

When the door opens again, Jase walks out. Willie is next.

"There he is," you say. "Luke Skywalker comin' to save the day."

"Luke? You kiddin' me? It's Han Solo. And that over there is Chewbacca." Willie points to Jase.

"What are you callin' me?" Jase says in his ornery sort of way.

Ah.

There's nothing like being home, Jack.

THE HAPPY END

TURN TO STONE

YOU LEAVE THE LIGHT-BLUE ROOM—something about it seems suspicious to you. As you head down a corridor, footsteps echo around you—from *both* directions.

Soon you see them. Pirates rushing toward you.

And hey, when will the idea of pirates in space ever sound cool or interesting? Because it ain't, and it's not hip to be square.

"Right here—there's a doorway!" John Luke shouts. You both run down a narrow hallway that ends in a round dead end of sorts.

You circle the enclosed space, trying to find any way out.

"Where are we?" John Luke asks.

Suddenly the floor drops out from under you, and you both fall while the ground underneath you lowers. It's like a really fast, messed-up elevator.

When the floor is steady again, you find yourself looking

up at the world from what appears to be a round pit somewhere in the bottom of the ship. Hissing sounds come from all around you as steam pours out from the walls.

There's no way to get out of this trap you're in. No way but up, of course.

Soon you can see two helmets peering down at you—one's silver and one's gold.

"Gentlemen, gentlemen, gentlemen," one of the masked men says.

"Hey, Jack. I'll show you a gentleman if you get down here and fight me one-on-one."

"Feeling warm, Silas? A bit hot, John Luke?"

"You'll be the hot one when I get out of here."

"I think we can cool you off a bit. How would you like a little brain freeze?" Gold Helmet asks.

The steam and smoke become more intense.

"We've never used this on humans, but it sure looks fun in the movies. Prepare the carbon freeze!"

As the hissing and fizzling accelerate all around you, John Luke gives you the saddest look you've ever seen.

"We'll be all right, John Luke."

"Uncle Si . . . I love you, man."

You smile. "I know."

Soon it's not so warm anymore. You feel a blast of cold air, then *really* cold air. Then you realize you can't move.

This is really unfortunate, too, 'cause they caught you right when you were picking your nose.

Carbon-encased nose-picking Si.

Not the best way to go out, Jack.

THE END

LOOK AT THE STARS

A Note from John Luke Robertson

I LOVE LISTENING TO MY FATHER TELL STORIES. He's always had an incredible gift to draw people in and make them laugh or surprise them. Obviously Dad got this gift from my papaw, Phil Robertson. Sitting in a duck blind between the two of them while they tell (or make up) stories has been a blessing growing up.

I've thought about this while working on these books. It's been both fun and challenging creating crazy story lines like the ones you just read. Anytime you start to fill a blank screen with words, there are many places where you can get it wrong.

But all I have to do is look up at the stars to realize that the very first Creator—*our* Creator—never gets it wrong. From the very beginning, when he created the sun and the moon and the stars, God got it right. And we see his endless creativity every morning at dawn and every evening at sunset.

The infinite reaches of the solar system show the awesome glory of our God. The fact that God could make something so endless and so truly out of this world boggles my mind. But it also gives me hope late at night when the darkness surrounds me. I just have to look up to see an ocean of stars and know God is in control.

I love Job 38:31-33, where God responds to Job's questions and doubts:

> *"Can you direct the movement of the stars—*
> *binding the cluster of the Pleiades*
> *or loosening the cords of Orion?*
> *Can you direct the sequence of the seasons*
> *or guide the Bear with her cubs across the heavens?*
> *Do you know the laws of the universe?*
> *Can you use them to regulate the earth?"*

Job's answer is the same as mine or anybody else's: no. Absolutely no way.

Yet God can and does. He doesn't need to ponder which choice to make like we do. His actions are always correct—even when we don't understand them.

Next time you look into space, think about Uncle Si being out there. No, just kidding. Really think about God's infinite creativity, as wide and deep as his infinite love for you and me.